THE GAMES KEEPER

THE SLIM HARDY MYSTERIES #3

JACK BENTON

AMMFA
PUBLISHING

THE GAMES KEEPER

1

THE KICK HURT.

Had it not been for the bucketful of booze he had drunk, it would have hurt a lot more, Slim thought as he doubled over, tensing the stagnant remnants of his military stomach muscles as the next kick came in.

'Stay away. I've told you. I won't tell you again.'

Fingers closed over the scruff of Slim's collar. A clenched fist rose, caught in silhouette by a street light. Slim braced for the impact, but when the punch came it didn't hurt as much as he had expected. He slumped to the pavement as his attacker cursed, shaking his hand.

That was the thing about faces. They were generally harder than the jostling bones of an untrained fist.

The man staggered away up the alley. Slim sat up, only for a metal rubbish bin lid to strike him in the side, followed by an upended refuse sack which rained stinking food matter over him, carrot peel and chicken skin sticking to his clothes and face.

'You want to eat our rubbish, be my guest. But if I catch you at it again, you'll find yourself in one of these bags. Got it?'

Slim, blinded by a paper bag of unidentified kitchen slops, nodded in what he hoped was the right direction. An overwhelming urge to say something sarcastic to rile the man further burned like an unreachable itch, but he resisted. A few seconds later the footsteps were gone. Slim pushed himself to his feet and stumbled back to the canal.

The Riverway Queen, the listing, derelict houseboat he now called home, appeared up ahead. Slim withdrew the key to the padlock he had bought with his last change and unlocked the door, moving the DANGER: KEEP OUT sign aside then propping it back up as he closed the door.

In the gloom he clicked the padlock shut through another loop on the inside then switched on the little paraffin lamp that hung from a hook in the ceiling.

The barge's downward, left-tilting angle had taken some getting used to. At the bottom end, a pool of water sloshed around the feet of a table and chairs, rising and falling with the changing depth of the canal, but most of the boat's insides were untouched. Nothing worked, but a fold-out sofa bed propped up on some sodden hardback books was comfortable enough, and there were plenty of cupboards to stock his booze.

He pulled off his clothes and dumped them into the dry sink. It was washing day tomorrow, especially now he had blood on his shirt. Rain was due in the morning, meaning tomorrow afternoon the canal would flow good and fresh. While he was used to smelling of musty damp and mulched plants—he washed both his clothes and himself in the canal, and soap was an unnecessary luxury—it always felt good to be truly clean.

He didn't look too good in the little mirror above the sink. The paraffin lamp left half his face in shadow, but one eye was badly swollen. His beard was flecked with blood and was long overdue a trim or removal altogether. He stood out too much, and that was never a good thing.

He remembered once an old friend telling him that the homeless were invisible, drifting by beneath the eyes of the world. Slim had found that not to be the case. In the six months since his eviction, he had been assaulted three times including tonight. Once had been done lazily by a group of likely lads strutting back from a nightclub with nothing better to do, and once with rather more ferocity by a group of other homeless for the sin of sleeping on someone's turf. Feet, fists, and even a piece of two by four used by one bearded shadow hadn't hurt as much as Slim had thought they might. Bodies healed, he found. The heart and its delicacies were far less resilient.

From a fridge that didn't work he took a beer that wasn't cold and popped the tab. It tasted bad—out-of-date because that was cheaper—but it took away a little of the pain.

Maybe tomorrow he would stop drinking again. He had stopped recently—less than two weeks ago he had quit for three days. It had gone so well he'd washed his suit and made it to the job centre to look for work.

Then something happened. He had seen someone who looked like someone else, or heard a voice that sounded like one of those which haunted him, and he'd found himself in a pub, drinking what was left of his unemployment money.

He opened the fridge again, looking at the dark line of cans. That he hadn't drunk them all, that he could keep a supply, it was surely a sign of control.

It wasn't all bad. There was still hope.

He sat down on the sloping sofa bench, feeling the uncomfortable creak of the boat beneath him. He'd been down worse than this before. He had to stay positive, and dream, if not hope, for something better.

He took a sip of the beer.

A buzzing near to his face woke him. Slim reached out to swat what he at first thought was a fly, but found his old Nokia phone under fingers numb from cold.

Despite his grogginess it amused him to find the phone charged in a houseboat with no power. Then he remembered an hour he had spent sitting in a MacDonald's toilet with his phone plugged into a wall socket hoping for a call back about a construction job.

The call hadn't come, and that had been, what, two, three days ago now? Slim forced a smile as he scrambled to press the answer button. It was a good thing he didn't get many calls.

'Hello?'

'Slim? Is that you? You sound like hell.'

'What's new? How are you, Kay?'

Slim's old army friend who now worked as a forensic translator laughed.

'I'm good, Slim. Same as ever. How are you really, Slim?'

'Not had the best week, but it's Sunday, isn't it? It all starts again tomorrow.'

'Slim, it's Monday.'

'Well, like I say, I'm not having the best of weeks.'

Kay laughed at the apparent joke. Slim just smiled at the phone while wishing his headache would clear.

'I wondered if you had a spot in your schedule,' Kay said.

Slim smiled at the irony. 'I can probably fit something in,' he said.

'I got a call from an acquaintance I knew from my last tour,' Kay said. 'He wants someone investigated for attempted blackmail.'

'He could call the police,' Slim said. 'It's not really my area of expertise.'

'He doesn't want the police involved,' Kay said. 'I know what you can do, Slim. I'm sure you can help.'

'What makes this case the kind of mess that would interest me?'

'The man to be investigated has been dead for six years. My contact wants to know how that's possible.'

Slim sighed. 'It's easy. Faked death, identity change. Happens all the time. How can your contact be sure the man is dead?'

There was a long pause, and Slim began to think

Kay had hung off. Then there came a quiet outtake of breath and Slim understood.

'Tell me, Kay. Believe me, there's not much I can't take. How does your contact know the man's dead?'

'Because he claims he killed the man himself.'

2

THE MAN WHO CALLED HIMSELF OLLIE OZGOOD didn't look like a murderer. With a smooth face hidden behind a thin, blond wisp of beard, he reminded Slim more of an Eastern European fisherman or the kind of cultured construction worker who operated heavy machinery at a quarry. He looked technically learned but not fiendishly clever enough to get away with murder. However, Slim knew well how looks could be deceiving.

Cold eyes watched every movement as Slim broke open three sugar sachets in turn and stirred them into coffee so thick it congealed on the spoon.

'You're an alcoholic?' Ozgood said.

'Recovering,' Slim replied. 'Nine hours dry. You have to start somewhere, don't you? Not the first time. I'm used to it.'

Ozgood nodded at the cup. 'You're swapping one addiction for another?'

Slim shrugged. 'Unless it tastes like it was brewed a week ago then left in the sun to dry, it's hardly a memorable experience.' He lifted the cup, took a sip and winced. 'Ghastly. Exactly how I like it.'

'When our mutual friend suggested you, I was expecting someone more to type.'

'I can wear a trench coat and a hat if need be,' Slim said. 'If you want me to smoke cigars I'll charge them as expenses. Now, I need to know why you think this man has come back from the dead.'

'I can't start from the beginning, because I'm not sure where the beginning is,' Ozgood said. 'To be on the safe side, I'll pick somewhere in the middle and work out from there.'

Slim nodded. 'Whatever you need to do.'

Ozgood turned in the chair, indicating the farmland beyond the terrace where they sat and the scattered houses that poked out of the green patchwork of fields as though they'd grown there from seeds.

'I'm the latest in a line of landowners. Almost everything you see belongs to me. And if it doesn't, it's not worth owning.'

Slim pointed at a grey spire sticking out of a stand of trees just down from the brow of the hill beyond the forested valley to the west.

'Even that church?'

Ozgood smiled. 'Firmly in the latter category. The current Sunday morning congregation numbers less than twenty, by all accounts. No money to be made there, but it keeps the locals happy. The extended churchyard, however, is rented land. My grandfather was a businessman, and bought up everything he could afford, certain one day its value would be revealed. He never saw the benefits, but my father maintained the estate, and since his death I've kept it running in his name. A cleverer man might have sold much of it off, but I remain confident that the current economic climes will improve before we're all ruined.'

Slim glanced up at the three floors of manor house rising above him and wondered if Ozgood had any real concept of what poverty meant. 'Kay said he knew you in the military,' he said.

Ozgood nodded. 'I was doing that typical hothead thing of trying to prove myself worthy. After two tours, I came to accept my family's inherited wealth would define me whether I liked it or not. Plus, I didn't appreciate getting shot at. What is it they say, that wars are fought by the poor to benefit the rich? Without being snobbish, I fall into the latter category.'

Slim smiled. 'And I the former.'

Ozgood's eyes never left Slim's face. 'Then we are both victims of circumstance. Like brothers … in arms.'

'We might have been if I had done better. I failed even at that.'

Ozgood's smile was colder than a chill wind off the sea. 'I so much prefer to work with vulnerable men. They're far easier to trust.'

'Watertight,' Slim said.

He looked back up again at the country house rising behind him in all its splendour. Ozgood Hall was the focal point for the two valleys falling away to either side. Set among twenty acres of landscaped gardens, it was the kind of place most people only visited on National Trust tours. Slim felt he had made a statement by bringing his own coffee.

'Plus,' Ozgood added, after a lengthy pause, 'I never liked the idea of killing someone.'

Slim deliberated over how to phrase his next question, but there was no point in trying to skirt around it. He knew about the murder, and Ozgood knew he knew.

'Yet you found out how it felt. The man attempting to blackmail you is supposedly dead by your own hand. Can you tell me about that?'

Ozgood leaned back in his chair and gave his chin a thoughtful rub. 'I wondered how soon you would ask, Mr. Hardy.'

'I believe in getting the worst out first,' Slim said. 'Then you can move on. Working for a murderer is a first for me, but a challenge I'm not in a position to refuse.'

Ozgood had winced at the mention of the word "murderer". Now he frowned, squeezed his eyes shut and rubbed his temples as though massaging a sudden headache.

Without looking up or opening his eyes, he said, 'I know all about your conviction.'

Slim lifted an eyebrow. 'Excuse me?'

Ozgood looked up, holding Slim's gaze until Slim wondered if he ought to look away. In the end, it was Ozgood who looked away first, but in a tired, nonchalant way that left Slim no sense of dominance, only that a noose had been removed from around his neck for a little while longer.

'I know that you were discharged from the military for attacking a man with a razor blade,' Ozgood said. 'He was supposedly having an affair with your wife. Is that right?'

'So I thought.'

'And you tried to kill him.'

Slim nodded. 'I failed. Luckily for both of us.'

'So before I tell you what I'm about to tell you, I want you to know that you have no moral high ground over me. Just to make that clear. It's one reason why I thought you'd be perfect for this case.'

'That's understood.'

'Good.' Ozgood shifted in his seat. He took a sip of his coffee and smiled. 'A man named Dennis Sharp lived and worked on my land. Specifically, he worked in forestry. I'd guess his job title was forest ranger, but he was more of an odd job man. He lived on my land and did whatever I asked. I thought he was a good man, and I trusted him. Then, one night just over six years ago, he assaulted my sixteen-year-old daughter.'

Slim just nodded. He lifted his cup and took a sip.

'It should have been dealt with by the police,' Ozgood said. 'At least initially. I'm a law-abiding man, after all. Unfortunately, the lag between the event and the investigation weighed in Dennis Sharp's favour.'

'What happened?' Slim asked.

'The case got thrown out, and Sharp thought he was a free man.' Ozgood sighed, leaned back into his chair and looked away into the distance. 'He wasn't. He never could be, could he? Not after what he had done.'

'So you took matters into your own hands?'

Ozgood lifted a finger to his lips and pouted, appearing to kiss it. He rubbed the base of his chin with his thumb. 'If you owe me, I will make you pay,' he said. 'Dennis Sharp made payment with his life.'

'How?'

'His car was looked over, a few adjustments made. His clutch failed coming through a turn on the steep road heading down into that valley you see over there.' Ozgood didn't point, but his head turned slightly, indicating a forested cleft beyond the farmland to the northwest. 'The car went off the road and struck a rock, killing him instantly, according to the coroner's report.'

'And you know he died?'

'An anonymous call was made to police, but it's not anonymous to the person who made it,' Ozgood said, rather cryptically, as though he was taking an active part in whatever game the blackmailer had decided to start. 'I was contacted by police, and I later viewed his body. I felt his neck for a pulse, just to be sure. Yet now, six years later, I've started to receive messages from a man claiming to be Dennis Sharp, demanding money, threatening to expose me, not just my part in his supposed death, but in other alleged crimes.'

Ozgood stood up, walked across to the terrace's edge, then turned and walked back again. Slim watched him, trying to make sense of this man. It was clear that Ozgood wasn't a man to be crossed, one whose amiable outer shell hid a steel-hard inner core.

'Let me be clear,' Ozgood said, turning and returning to his seat. He hooked one leg over the other, then changed his mind and sat back up straight, leaning forward. 'I do not fear this man dragging my name through the dirt. There is nothing he could have on me that could not be covered or disappeared. What disgusts me is the nerve of this person, which is why I have need of you to uncover his identity.' Ozgood leaned forward, his cold eyes making Slim uncomfortable. 'I consider this a personal slight against my family. In the right circumstances I might forgive such a thing against myself … but not against my daughter.'

Slim sipped his coffee, using it as an excuse to break Ozgood's gaze. 'It's most likely a case of stolen identity. Someone close to Sharp looking to squeeze something out of you.'

'There's no one who was close to Sharp who isn't dead or as good as.'

Slim wasn't quite sure how to respond to this statement, so he nodded in a show of agreement, letting his gaze wander slowly over the panorama of countryside while he waited for Ozgood to continue.

'This blackmailer knows things only Sharp could know.'

'And you want me to expose either the fraud or the circumstances that this man could be threatening you from?'

'That is exactly it. And when you discover the truth, I will either see him rot in prison or kill him all over again.'

3

Ozgood himself, carefully driving a pristine hatchback far too good for the road they were travelling, showed Slim to a small cottage that had once belonged to the estate's caretaker. It was along an old, meandering access road which had been replaced by a shorter lane to the property's rear, leaving the former access road to fall into disrepair. Unused now, the cottage was surrounded by forest at the bottom of a valley, approached by a barely discernible lane through trees which cut down one hillside, across a stream by a little bridge, before making a switchback outside the cottage. It then wound its way up the hill on the other side, in the direction of the small village where Slim had noted the church spire. As the road ascended steeply, cutting back on itself, Slim felt tired just looking at it.

With a pat on the back and a promise to be in touch, Ozgood left Slim alone, turning his car around with a scowl at the brambles by the roadside and then gingerly making his way back the way he had come.

The cottage looked unimpressive on the outside, with brambles grown up over one corner to dig their way into a roof space, and a crack in a front window, perhaps from a bird. However, it had electricity and hot water and a gas stove, and Ozgood had arranged for a weekly delivery of food in order to keep Slim catered for during the investigation.

There were also bugs hidden in a tabletop, in a skirting board in the cramped living room, and in a wooden statue of a fox in the bedroom. High quality, far newer and more expensive than Slim had ever used in the military or on previous cases, the kind that could record a pin drop or a sharp intake of breath.

Whatever the reason Ozgood felt he needed to keep tabs on Slim, Slim preferred to work in private, so he filled each receiver with Vaseline to muffle the sound to near inaudibility. It would take time for Ozgood to realise what had happened, perhaps enough for them to gain a trust in one another.

Slim, having returned to his sinking ruin of a squat long enough to fill two cases with everything he owned, packed his belongings away into a chest of drawers. Filling only the top two of three, he gave a shudder at how light and impermanent his life had become. He could disappear in an instant, leaving no trace.

Perhaps that was the plan. Slim wasn't naive enough to trust Ozgood fully, and the property baron clearly felt the same. It was a mutual distrust likely to benefit both.

Slim finished his unpacking and ventured outside. As

he closed the door, a rustling came from the trees to the cottage's side and a man stepped out onto the path.

Rheumy eyes looked up and a mostly toothless mouth smiled.

'Name's Croad,' the newcomer said. 'Boss told me to show you round.'

4

WEATHERED AS HE WAS LIKE AN OLD BARN ROOF, Croad was of indeterminable age, but, with a passion for Eighties football matches, Slim guessed his new guide to be around fifty.

'You know, I nearly made the bench at QPR back when Wilkins was just hitting his peak,' Croad said, baffling Slim that this limping tree stump of a man could have ever walked straight, let alone been good enough with a ball at his feet to get near a then-League One side.

'Strong squad they had back then or I might of made it. I'd scored ten in three games in the reserves, but celebrated me Saturday call up with a bottle of bourbon and a hussy I met in Soho. Bailed through a window when her husband rolled in late, ripped me hamstring on a railing fence then stepped in front of a 94 bus to Piccadilly. Might have been worse if it hadn't been slowing down to stop, but that was that.' He pointed. 'Ah, here's the ford. Road goes up to a junction. Left goes to the village, right to Weaton's farm, but stay away if it's raining as muck washes over the road and your car'll likely get stuck unless you have four-wheel drive.'

Slim was marvelling too much at the seamless transition from a tale of near-heroism to one of swollen rivers to mention that he had no current driver's license.

'Weaton's is still part of Ozgood's land but they have a long-term fixed lease so he has to keep his nose out.'

'What kind of a man is Mr. Ozgood?'

Croad shrugged. 'Is this on or off the record?'

'Off, of course,' Slim said, knowing full well anything he said would likely get back to his new boss one way or another. 'I mean, is he the kind of man who deserves to be blackmailed?'

'Depends who you ask. General rule, isn't it, that the more coin you have the longer the line of people wanting to steal it.'

Slim smiled. 'That's why I have so many friends.'

Croad emitted a gravelly laugh. 'You and me both.'

'I'm sure you know why I'm here. Mr. Ozgood wants to know why he's being blackmailed by a dead man.' Slim paused, remembering Ozgood's warning to say nothing about the true nature of Dennis Sharp's death.

'Aye. Dennis Sharp, never saw that coming. Quiet kind of guy, worked, got paid, went home or to the pub, the easy type.'

'I hear he died in a car crash.'

Croad nodded. 'Yeah.'

Slim waited for further information, but when none came, he said, 'Was it around here?'

Croad nodded. His incessant shuffle paused a moment and he turned back. 'Taking you there now. Master's request. Best to start at the beginning, isn't it?'

5

'DON'T GET THAT MANY SWITCHBACKS LIKE GUNHILL Hollow in these parts,' Croad said, waving at the road dipping abruptly out of sight over the brow of the hill as trees closed in around it like protective hands. 'I mean, you wouldn't expect that kind of curve to come on you if you were lost, driving this road for the first time.' Croad grinned, revealing cragged, blackened teeth. 'You'd take it easy, wouldn't you?'

'Of course,' Slim answered, not sure whether, after a drink of two, he would or not.

They walked on into the trees, the shadows slashing across them, the temperature dropping rapidly, the air dry from the afternoon sun turning dank and moist against Slim's skin.

The road narrowed and angled steeply, its surface potholed and uneven, shingly patches of broken tarmac crunching as they shifted underfoot. Slim had the uneasy sensation that he was walking across the acne-scarred face of a long dead and buried giant.

Croad stopped where the road abruptly cut back on itself, angling sharply downhill into the mossy green of the valley. He stepped into the verge and leaned forward, hands cupping his face.

'Yeah, she's still there.'

'She?'

'The old Ford. Sharp's wagon.'

Slim came forward. 'The car's still there?'

'What's left of it. Sharp hit this turn at real speed. Missed the largest trees and plunged a couple of hundred metres down into forest. They tried to tow line it out but what I heard was the line snapped twice and on the third time they couldn't be bothered. Police teams checked it for evidence, did their work on location, and then left it for anyone who might see.'

Slim peered downslope into the gloom beneath the trees. 'I can't see anything.'

'Not much left but a rusting hulk overrun by brambles, but she's there. Come on, I'll show you.'

Croad stepped off the verge, immediately dropping down as the hill fell away. Within a couple of steps he was below eye level. Slim's military drilling kicked in, and he squatted, scanning the undergrowth for anything that might be out of place, anything synthetic or human-altered.

A cackling laugh made him look up.

'Who are you, Schwarzenegger? Ain't nothing to worry about round here. This ain't 'Nam, soldier boy.'

Slim wondered how much of his past Croad knew, but he shrugged it off, grinning. 'Always loved the forest as a kid,' he said, something which while once true had been inverted since. He didn't like open spaces either, but at least you had a better chance of seeing your enemy.

'Didn't we all,' Croad said, turning and ambling off. 'Nothing to worry about except a few ghosts. They left the car but they took Den's corpse.'

Slim hurried after Croad, catching up as the old man came to a stop beside a tangle of undergrowth that suggested something hidden beneath. A little further on, a rocky outcrop jutted out of the earth and beyond it the bank dropped away into a stream channel.

'Front axle got lodged on that rock,' Croad said, stumbling through the undergrowth and slapping the outcrop with a surprisingly agile kick. 'Pigs did their investigation then left the car here to rot. Kids used to come down here and smoke skunk, call out old Den, see if he was still about.'

'They still come down here?'

'Got tired of cutting the weeds back, I think.' Croad grinned. 'Or they got spooked. More than a couple of kids sat in the hot seat and won't come in these woods no more.'

'The hot seat?'

Croad reached down and took hold of a clump of gnarled brambles with his bare hands, ripping them back to reveal a dirty, cracked side window. 'Front, driver's side. Where old Den met his maker.'

6

OZGOOD TOLD HIM THAT DURING HIS INVESTIGATION no question was unaskable of anyone living on his estate.

With a cup of coffee he had left standing in the filter overnight, Slim pored over large aerial photos of the area Ozgood had provided him with, matching the buildings and roads with those on an annotated map.

The photos stretched back thirty years, and in that time a couple of holdings had come and gone. Others, once standing in the open had become obscured beneath trees which had grown up, while others previously hidden now sat lonely and avoided among cleared areas or open gardens.

The manor house stood dead centre like a queen bee, surrounded by extensive gardens. These then segued into forest which gradually sloped down into two adjacent river valleys, turning Ozgood's estate into a diamond, although they never quite converged again.

Across the river to the northwest, the village of Scuttleworth stood, a cramped cluster of cottages surrounding a church, and bookended by two facing shops at one end, and a village green—in reality little more than a patch of scrubland Slim had seen during Croad's driving tour. The churchyard was the largest single land use, stretching over a couple of meadows separated by a line of trees, although north of Scuttleworth were a couple of industrial holdings: one grey block that looked like a factory perched on the edge of a valley, and the other an open grey space lined with parked cars and a couple of construction vehicles: a mechanic's yard.

On the edge of a smudge of trees a mile to Scuttleworth's south, Dennis Sharp's old cottage was highlighted with a double-ringed black circle and an annotation, in case Slim had been unsure. It lay along a meandering track which rose over the southern end of the western valley, wound through forest, and eventually connected with the old access road to Ozgood Hall.

Slim's current residence, the former caretaker's cottage, stood nearly halfway between the two, and was visible only as a brown smear through the trees. The old access road, clearly visible in a map dated 1971, was barely a dotted line on the most recent dated 2009, replaced by a new road to the east.

Slim counted fourteen other houses or homesteads not belonging to the manor estate or Scuttleworth. Two clusters were farms, while Croad had identified a line of three as former social housing Ozgood had bought up and now rented out. The others all belonged to various rent-paying locals.

Croad was waiting outside when Slim emerged, mouth sour from too much coffee but his mind—for once—feeling refreshingly sharp. He had begun to count the days of sobriety again as he always did. Four now without a drink, six since he'd got plastered and twelve since he'd woken up somewhere different to where he remembered going to sleep. The caffeine buzz was making his heart palpitate, but the gentle uncurling of the Ozgood case had aroused the curiosity only a bucketful of booze could bury. It was a web, for sure, but if he could somehow unravel it, he might actually get paid for once, and that eternal search for a meaning to his existence could be cooled for a while.

'You ready, boy?' Croad rasped. 'Got a busy day of stirring up some muck ahead of us.'

Slim nodded, inwardly sighing, wondering how long he would have to enjoy Croad's abrasive company before he could continue the investigation alone.

Croad had wheels too, an ancient Morris Marina which looked older than its owner. Faded green, it had one jarring chrome red door and a square of blue on the roof that looked to have been laid loose on top. Slim must have been staring because Croad suddenly cackled and said, 'Sunroof. Homemade. Air-con don't work.'

Slim considered saying something about windows but thought better of it. Instead he said, 'Where's our first stop?'

Croad grinned. 'Figured we'd get straight down to business. I'm taking you to see a ghost.'

7

As Croad's car bumped and bounced down country lanes Slim was sure hadn't been on his aerial maps, air pouring in through the roof hole as the blue painted board that usually covered the jagged opening jostled at his feet, Slim felt sure no one heading to meet a real ghost would pass the time talking about long forgotten games for Queens Park Rangers.

'Lad's name was Mickey,' Croad was saying, fingers drumming on the wheel. 'Ended up doing pretty well, won a cap for Scotland. But that day he showed up, he was the new kid on the training ground. Night before his first game for the reserves, we filled his boots with chili powder. Damp, misty day, it all got ground in like. Kid got scabies or whatever. Said his feet itched so much he practically scratched the skin off.'

'Scabies?' Slim muttered, feigning interest as Croad snorted with laughter.

'Kid would've got ruined if he hadn't been such a good sport about it … ah, here we are. Den's place.'

A gate overgrown with vines was set back from the road. The building behind—it was hard to tell it was a house—had boarded windows, but the front door had been kicked in and the entrance invaded by bushes and brambles. Slim got out of the car and approached the gate, only now seeing a second floor hidden among the branches.

'Den's place,' Croad repeated as he climbed out and came around the car to join Slim at the gate. 'After the first message arrived, Ozgood had me down here watching, see if Den showed up. Camped out for weeks. Nothing.'

'I thought Sharp was dead.'

'He is. Or he should be. Ghosts can't write letters or send emails though, can they?'

Slim made his way along the gate to a buried stone wall and climbed over. If there had once been a semblance of a garden it was long gone, replaced by a vicious thicket of brambles which clutched at Slim's jeans as he kicked his way through.

'You going inside?' Croad asked. 'You'll need this.' He leaned over the gate to hand Slim a torch. 'Kids trashed the place so Ozgood got it boarded up, since it was only ever leased.'

'I'd like to meet these kids,' Slim said. 'I imagine they have stories to tell.'

'Down the green on a Friday night,' Croad said. 'You'll find them out in the beer garden, drinking cheap cider. Keep Cathy's shop in business, they do.'

Slim nodded. He took the torch and angled it into the gloom. The outlines of decomposing kitchen units appeared through the matting of vegetation. Treading carefully, he moved a few steps inside, but there was nothing to see except the ruined cottage. Shattered glass, chips of masonry and a few unidentifiable pieces of metal provided a base layer to the usual suspects of an abandoned property: a few crushed cans of Special Brew, a couple of damp, torn porno magazines, and a dusty used condom which had split at the duty end.

At his shoulder, Croad said, 'I take responsibility for the cans. The rest, I have no claim.'

Slim switched off the torch. 'No one lives here,' he said. 'I think it's time we stopped all the sightseeing and someone told me about the nature of this supposed blackmail.'

Croad grinned. 'You're the boss. You want it inside the car or out?'

8

A FEW MINUTES LATER THEY SAT IN THE FRONT OF Croad's old Marina, flask cups of coffee on their laps. Croad pulled out a sheet of paper and passed it across to Slim who balanced it on his knees as he read.

'First one,' Croad said.

'Dear Oliver,' Slim read. 'I'll get straight to the point. You might be surprised to hear from me, but I'm not dead as you must have hoped. I apologise for that. In fact, the tragedy you believe befell me never actually happened. I'm very much alive. I'm alive but rather frustrated. That's where you come in. You see, I know what you did, and I think it's time you paid up. I also know about everything else. I'll be going to the police if you don't do exactly as I ask. Yours, Dennis.'

The note closed with a request for half a million pounds in cash to be left in a bag on an overpass across the nearby A30 duel carriageway. The date and time: September 6th at 7.15pm.

Slim scoffed as he handed it back. 'Standard blackmailer fare,' he said. 'Not a single concrete detail. I'm assuming it was ignored.'

'Course,' Croad said. 'Mr. Ozgood's a businessman. Gets letters like this every day. This one never made it past his secretary. So the blackmailer got a little more specific.'

'Show me.'

'Here's the first one passed to Ozgood himself.'

Slim took the sheet of paper and began to read, silently this time.

Dear Oliver,
I noted that you didn't show up on September 6th.
Not like you to miss an important date, is it?
I don't think you realise I'm serious.
I know what you did. Do you think your
money will get you off? Yeah, well it did.
Lucky you. No such luck for the less privileged.
The asking price is now one million.
That might repair some of the damage you caused.
Tell Ellie when you see her,
that I'll never forget her smile
when she told me that she loved me.
And ask her about that scratch on her back.
The bramble ... I didn't know it was there.
Your shadow until I see your money,
at 6 o'clock on October 2nd,
the same place as before.
Dennis

Slim looked up. 'I'm guessing Ozgood took this one a little more seriously?'

'Not wrong,' Croad snorted. 'During the alleged rape, Ellie Ozgood was scratched on her back, just like Den's letter claims. There was a trace of thorn in her skin, and forensics in the initial investigation actually traced it back to the exact plant in Den's garden.' Croad pointed. 'Right through there, though it's grown up a bit since. It would have been enough to convict him had Ellie not pulled her charges.'

'She what? Ozgood told me the case got thrown out.'

'Yeah, bit of a sore point with him, that. Ellie dropped the case. Claimed it was consensual. Girl was a month past her sixteenth birthday, putting Den in the clear. He was thirty-eight. Mr. Ozgood didn't like it, didn't believe her or Den. Couldn't have his little girl playing round with the gardener, see? So he took matters into his own hands.'

'So I gathered.'

Croad grinned, but for the first time it had taken on a sinister angle. In the gloomy half light through the trees the old man's face became skeletal, threatening.

'The three musketeers,' he said.

'What?'

'There's just us three what know about what Ozgood did that night. Him, course, me, and now you. I owe him a life debt, and you do now too. There ain't no telling, that clear?'

Slim decided not to mention that it appeared Ozgood himself had broken his sacred circle by boasting of his deed to Kay Skelton. Instead, he said, 'Are you threatening me?'

'Just establishing me parameters. I been on the staff a while, earned me trust. You less so. I don't consider no debt paid, so let's be clear who you's working for.'

Slim took a deep breath. The temptation to walk away was strong, but so was the lure of the nearest pub, and perhaps more likely to get him killed.

'I understand,' he said.

'Good. Now, there's more. There's always more, isn't there?'

Slim frowned, unsure to what Croad was referring, but the old man passed him another sheet of paper.

'Third and final one,' he said.

Dear Oliver,
This is your last chance to settle up. Don't
forget what you did to Scuttleworth, or
how many lives you destroyed.
It is time for you to pay for
the hurt you caused. I've given you
a chance to help me make amends.
9th November, 5.25pm.
A black leather bag tied to the ninth pillar.
See you then,
Dennis

Slim passed back the letter. 'You know the questions I'm going to ask, don't you?'

Croad grinned. 'Knife sharp, me. That came eight days ago. We have just over two weeks until payday. All that business about turning Mr. Ozgood in, he don't know what it's about. Nothing but threats and lies. It's the girl who's the problem, though.'

'Ellie? Why?'

'Mr. Ozgood wants to ship her out, get her out of harm's way.'

'But?'

'Stubborn ass mule won't leave. Said she ain't worried about no threats from no one. Makes you think, don't it?'

'Does Ozgood plan to leave the money?'

'Not if he can help it. That's why you're here.'

'I don't work particularly fast,' Slim said. 'I'm not sure I can save his money.'

Croad laughed. 'You think Mr. Ozgood cares about a couple of mil? You don't get it yet, do you? No one crosses Mr. Ozgood. Dennis Sharp did once and got himself dead. Whoever is sending these letters will go the same way. You're here to keep the blood off Mr. Ozgood's hands, or at least keep it to a level where it can be easily washed away.'

9

CROAD MADE AN EXCUSE ABOUT OTHER DUTIES THEN dropped Slim back at the cottage, leaving him little wiser than before. On the surface it seemed clearly a case of stolen identity. If the evidence was as he had heard it, there had to be some mistake about Dennis Sharp still being alive. The blackmailer was someone no doubt close to the family who knew more than Croad realised. All Slim needed to do was catch the person and expose him. Then Ozgood could return to world domination and Slim to his gradual descent into a grimy, forgettable death.

Croad had given him a scribbled list of contacts, adding a star next to those most likely to talk. In annotated notes at the bottom, he explained that a cross meant they would likely tell Slim to get lost.

The first name on the list was Clora Ball. Croad's notes described her as "Looks old, smells bad, doesn't smile. Den's ex-girlfriend."

Her address was a twenty-minute walk down a narrow lane, ending at an awkward two-storey building in which the lower floor was used as a farm vehicle storage. Clora lived on the upper floor, accessed through a door around the building's side. Slim found himself pressing a button on a modern door control with no idea what he would say.

'What?' came an electronic voice through a receiver. 'Do you know what time it is?'

Slim glanced at the display on his old Nokia phone. 9.45 a.m.

He told her the time. 'Can I speak to you, please? I'd like to ask you about Dennis Sharp.'

The receiver clicked off. Slim waited for long seconds, thinking he'd already reached a dead end, when the door clicked, popping open a couple of inches.

'Up here!' a voice shouted down from a door at the top of a steep staircase.

Slim went up. The smell hit him halfway. The familiar pungency of a life discarded: old takeaways, cigarettes, stale booze. He paused, waiting for his head to stop pounding, aware his investigation could be unraveled on its first day, and then continued up.

Clora Ball had retreated to an armchair throne in the midst of a kingdom of junk. The elements of a regular life existed in kitchen units, cupboards, tables and chairs, but it looked as though a wave had come through, depositing junk on every available surface. She picked up a TV remote and pointed it at a TV not immediately obvious amidst a stack of boxes, then turned to look at him in defiance as an episode of *Trash Wars* ironically began to play.

'You didn't give me a chance to tidy up. Who are you anyway?'

'My name is Slim Hardy. I'm a private investigator. I wanted to ask you about an old acquaintance. Dennis Sharp.'

'Well, that's a story, isn't it? Haven't heard that name in a while, not that it's one you could ever forget.'

Clora, for all her outward elusiveness, appeared happy to have company. When Slim didn't immediately respond, she flapped a chubby hand at an adjoining kitchen.

'I just boiled one,' she said. 'Bring me one if you're making. If you wanted to kill me you'd have done it by now so I guess you mean me no harm.'

Slim dutifully picked his way to the kitchen and returned with two cups of tea. The milk had soured so he left his black and added just a dribble to Clora's.

He cleared a seat and sat down nearby.

'You forgot the sugar,' Clora said, as though Slim should have known. 'I guess I should cut back so I'll let it go. You know Den's dead, don't you?'

Slim feigned surprise, then began to set down the elaborate lie he had constructed to encourage people to talk.

'I'm working on behalf of an investment fund based in London,' he said. 'Mr. Sharp had some assets which have matured. The fund manager was unable to contact him so sent me to track him down, and in his absence, his next of kin.'

'How much money?'

'Middle six figures,' Slim said, watching as she looked up at the ceiling, frowning as she tried to calculate how much that might be. 'It's a significant sum. The terms of the agreement are that it should pass into the hands of his next of kin in the event of his lawful death. A chap I met in the village gave me your address.' He shifted on the seat, preparing to cast the hook that would land her. 'The fund manager has authorised minor payments to anyone able to offer reliable information.'

'How much?'

'It varies. How well did you know Mr. Sharp?'

Clora shifted. The chair creaked beneath her, the floorboards too. Flabby arms lifted as though holding out information and she grinned.

'We were lovers.'

'You were in a relationship with Mr. Sharp?'

Clora shrugged. 'Hardly. He was a rogue, was Den. I wasn't the only one and I knew it, but I didn't care.' She smiled again, her eyes far away. 'He was that bit of rough that a woman couldn't resist. I wouldn't have cared if he was bonking half the village as long as he came back to me from time to time.' Her countenance suddenly darkened. 'But when I heard about Eleanor, he crossed a line.'

'Eleanor? Ellie Ozgood? Oliver Ozgood's daughter?'

'You've done your research,' Clora said. 'Ozgood's daughter and heiress.'

'They had a relationship?'

'So people said. Found it hard to believe. Den was in

his thirties. Might have appealed to a certain age group, but to a rich public school girl … couldn't see it myself. Then all that with the rape came out. Made more sense.'

'Of course you were shocked by what he did?'

'The rape?' Clora laughed. 'A load of rubbish, all that. Den was no rapist, didn't have it in his nature.' She smirked. 'With that look in his eyes, didn't need to be. No, her word against his. Case would have been thrown out even if her charge weren't withdrawn. Den was cleared of any wrongdoing, as anyone with half a brain knew he would be. No, he crossed a line by going near her in the first place. By going with the enemy.'

10

SLIM HAD HOPED FOR MORE ELABORATION, BUT CLORA
had abruptly announced that a quiz show she liked was
about to start and that Slim should come back another
time if he wanted to talk more.

Back outside, he walked up the lane to the junction,
taking the direction which led into the village of
Scuttleworth, his head rattling with new ideas. Supposed
to be finding out who might have had the knowhow to
impersonate Dennis Sharp, he found himself drawn to
veiled accusations of impropriety on behalf of Ollie
Ozgood and his family.

Scuttleworth straddled a crossroads, clustered and
crouched like the spider its name suggested, although
only the northern road could be considered suitable for
traffic. All roads south of the church degraded into
mostly single-lane tracks, cutting back and forth across
the valleys and hills as though once-upon-a-time a giant
had laid a loose string net haphazardly across the

landscape. The road to the north held the few commercial buildings—two small shops, a post office and an adjacent builder's merchants. A church was set into a dip and surrounded by trees, across the road from a pub. The east-west road was two facing rows of cramped stonewalled cottages that gradually gave way to farmland.

No one was about. One of the two shops was shut, a cardboard sign up in its window which had faded in the sunlight to illegibility. Slim went into the other, pushing through a door half blocked by a green raincoat lying on the floor, and finding himself in a long, tight room narrow enough that he could simultaneously reach over the shelves to touch the walls on either side. Baring a rack amply stocked with two-litre bottles of distilled water, the shop didn't have much of anything. Slim picked up a tin of beans, turned it over to reveal a best before date two months past. A packet of dried noodles was the same, while a loaf of granary bread in a basket by the till was stale—hard to the tentative touch of Slim's finger.

'Can I help you?'

Slim, running a finger through the dust along the counter edge, jumped at the voice. It came from below him. He leaned over the counter and found a boy in shorts sitting cross-legged on the floor with a handheld game console flickering in the space between his legs. The boy wore no shoes or socks, and a faded blue t-shirt showed pale skin through moth holes in the shoulders.

'Um … I was looking for newspapers,' Slim said, picking the first thing that came to mind.

The boy rolled his eyes as though such a request was preposterous. He looked back at his game a moment, then, as though realising the conversation wasn't over, looked up and said, 'Got one you want to order? I can ask Mum.'

'Where is your mother?'

The boy didn't turn. 'In the back room.'

'What's she doing?'

'How would I know?'

The conversation was turning into inanity, so Slim took a packet of pasta off a shelf and dropped it unceremoniously on the counter.

'I'll take this, please.'

The boy sprang into action, leaping to his feet and hollering, 'Mum!' through a curtain pulled over the entrance behind.

The creak of old sofa springs, the dragging of slippers over linoleum, and a long sigh announced the lady of the house before she pushed through the curtain. She saw the pasta before she saw Slim, then pushed fat rimmed glasses up her nose and looked up.

Whatever attractiveness youth might have given her had long been snatched away by the passing of time. A thick, shapeless body hid behind a grey sweater with a rip on one arm. Grey eyes peered out of a face that had too much skin and a mouth with two slugs for lips parted to reveal the glimmer of a silver molar.

'Are you Cathy?' Slim asked, remembering something Croad had said, and hoping the old man hadn't been referring to the closed shop across the road.

If the woman was surprised, there was no sign of it

in her face. 'Who are you?' she asked, looking away from him, absently tidying a wicker basket on the counter filled with cans of sweet corn. A luminous pink star propped up at the front announced an autumn half-priced sale.

'I'm staying in the area for a few days,' Slim said, avoiding the main thread of the question. 'Actually, I'm looking for Dennis Sharp. Or I was, but I heard he's passed away.'

'That's a polite way to put it. What did you want him for?'

'It's personal. I'd rather not say.'

She shrugged. 'Your business. A pound ten for that.'

She shoveled the pasta off the counter into a paper bag. Slim searched in his pocket for change, making a show of it to buy himself some time. Finally withdrawing a couple of coins, he said, 'Was Dennis well liked around here?'

'Why do you care if he's dead?'

'Wondering, that's all.'

'There are worse people you could meet, I suppose. Always had a joke, did Den, even if he was a bit free with his hands.'

'What does that mean?'

The woman nudged the boy in the back with her knee. 'Get back there, make yourself useful. Clean the floors or something.'

As the boy scrambled off, she turned back to Slim and gave him a warmer smile than he might have thought she was capable of. 'Liked the ladies, he did. Shouldn't have ever gone near that girl.'

'What girl?'

'Ellie Ozgood. He was never satisfied with anything easy, was Den. He went looking for trouble and he couldn't have looked for it in a better place.'

'I'd very much like to meet her. Do you know where she lives?'

'Up the Hall of course. But good luck getting in there. You're more likely to find her at work, if you could say her lording over that place is work. My Tom is always complaining about her, says she does nothing but sit on her fat—' Cathy cut herself off. She brushed a hand through her hair, tucking a greasy strand behind her right ear. 'Well, I guess that's enough of that.'

'What place?'

'You been living under a bucket? Vincent's. The abattoir. Second turning on the right past ours. Don't worry if you miss it, you'll smell it from a mile off.'

11

'Vincent's? No need for you to be going in there,' Croad said, sitting across the table from Slim. 'Do I need to remind you who hired you?'

'I was told Ellie Ozgood worked there. If anyone's spoken to Dennis Sharp, it's her.'

Croad shook his head. 'Mr. Ozgood wants Ellie left out of this. He doesn't want the assault dredged up all over again.'

'But—'

'Save it, Mr. Hardy. I'm just the messenger but these is the rules of the job. Take it or leave it.'

Slim wanted to get up and walk away, but memories of listing houseboats and swinging boots made this place safe … for now.

'As you say,' he said. 'Do something useful, won't you? Get me a list of people with a connection to Dennis. Family, friends, acquaintances.'

Croad grinned. 'You only had to ask.' He pulled a

crumpled piece of paper out of his pocket and laid it on the table, his crusty workman's fingers doing their best to smooth it out.

'That should do you.'

It looked like a spider's web of child's handwriting. Slim stared it, hoping something legible or cognitive would make itself known. When nothing happened, he looked up at Croad.

'Perhaps you could explain this to me,' he said.

Croad jabbed a finger at a scribble that could have read anything.

'Shelly Holland. Den's mother.'

'Remarried?'

'Never was. Wedlock. Den took his dad's name just to spite her.'

'Oh. Where will I find her?'

Croad stood up. He waved a hand at Slim's jacket hung over the back of a chair and headed for the door.

'Taking you there now. If she's still there.'

They took Croad's car, but it was less than two minutes before they were getting out again, Croad parking up on an overgrown verge outside the churchyard. A line of old cottages faced them across a gravel driveway dotted with weeds, more rundown than Slim would have expected for such potentially lucrative properties.

'Ozgood owns these too?' Slim asked.

Croad waved them off with a dismissive hand. 'All of them. Tenants in three. Fourth lot ran off after a year. Six months in arrears.'

'I bet that went down well.'

'Those of us accountable weren't best pleased, but for Mr. Ozgood it was nothing more than a flea bite on his backside.'

'The other three?'

'Work at Vincent's, like most round here.'

'That's Ozgood's primary source of income?'

Croad shrugged. 'One of them. You want to meet Shelly or not? This way.'

Croad led them up the steps to the churchyard gate. Slim paused as Croad pulled the gate out of entangling weeds and held it open.

'I thought she was alive.'

'She is. Last time I looked.'

The churchyard was wildly overgrown. Slim wondered if maintaining it was another of Croad's duties and whether it was worth calling the old man on it. Ancient, listing stones appeared out of the swaying seed heads of long grass, lichen-crusted inscriptions barely legible.

'Doesn't look like anyone comes here,' Slim said.

'They don't. Not anymore. Not a lot of people round here means not a lot of deaths. Den was one of the most recent and he's six years' buried already.'

'Where is he?'

'You'll see.'

The path wound around the church's rear, then branched off, heading over a low rise towards a line of trees separating it from a second, adjoining churchyard which looked more like a small field tacked on to deal with overflow. Slim tried to see past Croad to where the path went. He could only assume it cut right across the churchyard to a small estate on the other side, although he could see nothing except more fields.

'Isn't there a quicker way through?' he asked Croad. 'It looks pretty overgrown.'

'We're not going through,' Croad said. 'We're going just up here.'

They passed through the line of trees. The secondary churchyard was a field after all. A line of fresher graves stood near the trees, but the rest of the field was untended. The path died a few metres out, buried by grass.

'Careful of that,' Croad said, as Slim nearly tripped on an electrical extension cord snaking through the grass. 'One of the local do-gooders hooked her up with power.'

Slim frowned, questions forming on his lips, but Croad had already marched on ahead. Slim, wishing he'd worn waterproof trousers, picked his way more carefully in pursuit.

A few paces further along, Croad stopped. 'Here we are,' he said. 'Smells like cooking's going on. Mean's she's home.'

Slim stared. The field sloped away towards a trickling stream. Halfway there, a green tarpaulin poked up out of the grass, supported by haphazard poles, some of which had broken through the plastic, which had then been patched up with packing tape. As they got closer, Slim saw one was a piece of old wood still with bent nails rusted into its grain, while another was actually part of a low-hanging tree branch, lifting and falling with the sough of the wind.

Up ahead, Croad stopped. He turned back to Slim with a jagged grin on his face.

'Are you ready for this?' he asked.

'For what?'

'Ex-military, aren't you? Well, get ready to take cover. Bombs are about to start dropping.'

Slim gave the sky an involuntary glance. Croad took a step forward and shook the edge of the tarpaulin. It gave a crusty rustle and several handfuls of accumulated leaves fell free.

'Shelly? You in there? It's Croad. Brought someone who wants to ask about Den.'

From inside came a crunching sound like someone walking over dried newspaper. A corner of tarpaulin was thrown open to reveal a wild, ancient face framed by grey-blonde curly hair pushing out from beneath a blue bandana. Eyes narrowed and her lips drew back in a feral snarl. Hissing, she snapped at Croad, and then swung a stick at him. He took a step back out of the way, lifting his hand.

'We're all peaceful here,' he said. 'This here's Mr. Hardy. Wants to ask about Den. Old school friend, wasn't it?'

Slim made no effort to reply. Shelly turned her snarl on him, grime on her cheeks cracking and peeling off. She pursed her lips, appearing to blow him a kiss, and then she spat, a globule of mucus landing just short of his shoes.

'Get away from here,' she snapped, her voice husky and crackly, a sign of heavy cigarette or liquor abuse, or both.

'I'm looking for Dennis Sharp,' Slim said.

Shelly reached behind her as though searching for something to throw.

'Fool thinks Den's still alive,' Croad snapped. 'Show him, Shelly, so he'll leave me alone.'

'Get off my damn porch, you weasel,' she spat at Croad, making him take another step back. 'I used to like your smile but you've had it so far up Ozgood's backside for so long it's filled up with—'

'I can come back at a better time,' Slim said.

Shelly snarled and tossed something at him. It hit his thigh and bounced away. Slim frowned. A handmade doll, dirty and scuffed as though someone had dragged it along concrete with their foot. A head made out of shaped wire had little depressions and a glue residue where its eyes had been gouged out, while its mouth was covered by masking tape. With a frown, Croad lifted a foot and kicked it away into the grass.

'Just show him, Shelly,' the old man said. 'Let him see it.'

Shelly threw a barrage of swear words at Croad, but stepped back a little and nudged something hidden under the tarp with a dirty, frayed shoe.

A little wooden cross.

'My boy's right here,' she snapped. 'Right here with me, where he should be. Where no one can do him no harm no more. Now get out of here and don't come back.'

12

SLIM WAS TOO TRAUMATISED BY THE VISIT WITH Shelly to speak as Croad drove back to the cottage. There was too much he would never forget—the woman's wild eyes, the broken doll, and the little cross, strung with daisy chains which could have been made by a child.

'You had enough for one day?' Croad asked as he pulled up outside. 'You get much from her? She hiding him, you think?'

Slim just shrugged. He nodded goodbye to Croad then climbed out and went inside, feeling a sense of relief as the car drove off.

For the first time in a couple of days he had a desperate craving for a drink, and sat at the table with his head in his hands, waiting for the feeling to pass.

Croad had brought him more lists, and as soon as he was able, he called a man named Evan Ford, whose name had DI in brackets beside it, followed by a note that said "in case you wanna check Den's really dead".

Ford agreed to meet Slim in the nearby village of Stickwool. Reluctant to have Croad accompany him, Slim hiked out to the main road, where he was lucky enough to wave down a passing local bus which dropped him off on the village's outskirts.

Ford wore a light walking jacket and carried a stick over his knees. His hair stuck up in clumps, and oversized glasses made him look like a police officer failing poorly to go undercover. He stood up to shake Slim's hand then hailed the lone waitress for two coffees before Slim could even see a menu.

'I heard I might get a call from you at some point,' Ford said by way of greeting. 'You're the one asking about Dennis Sharp? Something about an inheritance.'

'It's a small amount,' Slim said, suppressing a sigh, feeling a growing frustration at his charade and Croad's ability to get in ahead of him anywhere he might be able to ask some decent questions.

'And you need proof of his death before you can pass it off to his next of kin?'

'Something like that.'

Ford produced a plastic envelope. 'I have a copy of his death certificate,' he said. 'It's not the original, I'm afraid. That's kept at the public records office. You could view it if you made an appointment.'

'I'm sure that won't be necessary.' Slim looked over the document, feigning interest. It could easily be faked if he were at the centre of some bizarre conspiracy, but what would be the point?

'You were the officer in charge of the investigation?' Slim said, pushing the document back across the table and looking up. 'Could I ask if there was any sign of foul play?'

Ford shook his head. 'None. Dennis Sharp's accident had all the hallmarks of a man driving too fast on a road he knew too well, getting cocky and making a mistake in poor driving conditions, a mistake that cost him his life.'

Slim leaned forward. 'And there was no tampering to the car?'

'It was an old car. Sharp wasn't a wealthy man. Half a dozen things could have gone wrong on that car at any time. But were there obvious signs of foul play?' Ford shook his head. 'The investigation found none.'

'I heard Sharp had recently been acquitted of a sexual assault on Ellie Ozgood, the daughter of a local landowner.'

'Acquitted, no. It never went to trial. The girl withdrew her charge.'

'I heard a rumour they were in a relationship.'

'What does that have to do with an inheritance?'

'Well,' Slim said, 'if a child had come out of their relationship, it would mean a whole lot.'

Ford shook his head. 'I think you'll be looking elsewhere for a next of kin.'

Slim nodded at the envelope. 'What else do you have?'

'Croad told me you would be persistent. Are all inheritance lawyers like you?'

Slim suppressed a smirk. 'Oh, we're sharks.'

'I think his mother is his only living relative. We tried

to contact the father listed on Dennis's birth certificate, Julian Sharp. However, it was found he had died in the mid-nineties. Dennis had a younger brother too, but he is also deceased.'

Slim frowned. Death seemed to follow Dennis Sharp like a sun shadow. 'I've met his mother,' he said. 'Without an official analysis, I'd gather that she is not of sufficiently sound mind to handle a trustee account. Are there no other siblings? Cousins? Perhaps a brother or sister born out of wedlock that was given up for adoption?'

Ford frowned. 'That's a strange thing to say.'

Slim shrugged. 'I'm not convinced, that in these parts, there could be no blood relative besides a mother.'

'Something of a snobbish attitude, don't you think? You're implying that country folk do nothing but breed.'

Slim learned forward, preparing his most condescending tone, aware it would sufficiently seal his masquerade as a city lawyer. 'But don't they?'

Ford stood up. 'I think we're done, Mr. Hardy. I hope my information was useful.' Then, with his face turned theatrically upwards, he marched out.

13

DESPITE CROAD'S WARNINGS, AFTER CATCHING A BUS back to Scuttleworth, Slim hiked up through the village. He climbed over a stile on to a public footpath, hiking uphill until he got his first sighting of the abattoir. Far from the crumbling shed of animal suffering and death he had always imagined of such places, it was a clean and compact industrial holding surrounded by an asphalt car park and ringed by a tall wire fence.

The years of hard drinking had laid waste to Slim's old army physique, but his eyes were still good enough to make out the rectangular boxes on top of poles that had to be CCTV cameras. Objectively he didn't blame them; the threat of intrusive activists was everywhere now, no matter how humane or ethical their production process was. Slim had nothing against animal rights, but would as soon as eat a steak as pet a cow on the head.

Still, big business was big business. And whether yours was cutting animals into slices or filing financial slices off pension schemes, it was rare to find a corporation without a skeleton hiding in a closet somewhere.

Slim pulled out his Nokia and unfolded a piece of paper tucked into his phone case behind the handset. A list of old army contacts, all those who'd gone on to achieve something yet didn't hate his guts. Platoon brotherhood was tighter than blood, and he'd deposited a couple of favours over the years. In return he'd done what he could to work off his debts: exposing a cheating partner for one, establishing a retirement fund for another, even helping erect a shed for a third.

He called up Donald Lane, an old friend from the military who had set up an intelligence consultancy in London after leaving the armed forces. Donald specialised in working with the police and the government, but had helped Slim out on previous cases in the past.

'Don, it's Slim. Been a few months, you good?'

'Slim? Good to hear from you, mate. I'm me, as always. Are you still you? Holding it together?'

Slim smiled. 'Actually, the best in a while. Don, I need a background check done on a company.'

'That all? Easy. What are you looking for?'

'At this stage, I'm not sure. It might have nothing at all to do with my investigation, but then again it could be a cornerstone. You can't tell, can you?'

'So you're after anything, then? Rumours, accusations, tabloid stuff, that kind of thing?'

'That's about it. You get bingo if you come up with any filed lawsuits. Anything that suggests some kind of wrongdoing. I'm looking for the kind of stuff that might have leached out into the surrounding community. Caused hard feelings, created grudges. That kind of stuff.'

'Leave it with me. I know a man who works in the financial press who has his ear to the ground. I'm guessing this is top secret?'

'Say no more than you have to. I'm in the employ of a dangerous man. The problem I have is not knowing how dangerous.'

Don laughed. 'How do you get yourself into these spots?'

Slim couldn't help but grin. 'I have to take what I get offered. Perhaps it's time I updated my website.'

'Last time I checked, you didn't have one.'

'That's what I mean.'

Slim gave Don the details, then thanked him and hung up. He pulled another piece of paper from the back of his phone case and smoothed it out. In far better condition than the other, this was his recently written schedule of tasks.

Croad had drawn up a list of pretty much everyone within a five mile radius who might have crossed paths with Dennis Sharp at some point. Slim had narrowed it down to the ten people most likely to know something, but it was a vague list at best and still far too broad. Slim felt like he was being asked to carry out the kind of investigation a police force would assign to a whole team. If he wanted to discover the mysterious blackmailer's true identity, he had to move fast, and he felt like he was treading in quicksand.

It didn't help that the one person who might know something—Ellie Ozgood—was seemingly off-limits.

Slim frowned. He felt like someone was pranking him, as though he was waiting for Jeremy Beadle to jump out from behind a tree and scream 'surprise!' while cackling with laughter.

The blackmailer was threatening to expose Ozgood. But expose what?

It could hardly be Sharp's murder. If so, it would be far safer and make more sense to go to the police, somewhere upcountry perhaps, where Ozgood had no influence.

No, it had to be personal.

But what?

14

CROAD LEANED AGAINST THE DOORFRAME, HANDS IN his pockets, one finger poking out of a hole and playing with a frayed seam of his jeans.

'I'll ask.'

'I want everything he has. I know he killed a man, Croad. What could be worse? I need to know what Dennis Sharp is threatening to reveal.'

At the mention of the murder, Croad's eyes had lifted, flicking around the room as though looking for cameras or microphones.

'You've been warned to watch what you say,' he said slowly, a hint of menace creeping into his voice.

'I can't hunt for a dead man if I'm barred from all the best leads,' Slim said.

'I'll see what I can do,' Croad said. He went out without another word. The front door slammed, then a moment later Croad's car started up, the engine squealing as he drove quickly away.

Slim had the urge to walk out of the door and never come back, to leave Ollie Ozgood and his troubles behind. But it was too late. Withdrawing with the secrets he already knew would never be allowed.

He went back out on foot, this time working himself up into a light jog as he headed through the tangle of lanes in the direction of Dennis Sharp's wrecked car. It felt strange to jog after so many years. Something he had once taken as a daily given felt cumbersome and unfamiliar, and before long he was sweating profusely, breathing hard even at the earliest sign of an incline. Long before he reached the top of the first hill he had given in, leaning on a gate nearly buried by the hedgerows either side, looking up at the steep slope of a field rising in furrows to the grey sky overheard.

And from nearby came voices.

'I'm not sure, Jim. I mean, I don't know—'

'Don't worry about it. Just close your eyes and breathe. It'll relax you.'

'Jim, I'm not sure—'

'Would I even ask if I didn't know it was safe? Would I? Come on, I've done it loads of times.'

'I don't know….'

'Come on … hey!'

Slim realised the gate had creaked beneath his weight. He stepped back, but too late.

'Who's there?'

A rustle of undergrowth came from inside the hedgerow. They were just out of sight. Too late to hide himself, Slim decided to show his face. He climbed onto the gate's lowest slat but it splintered and broke. His foot splashed down in a muddy puddle.

'Who's that? You some perv? I'll have you if you are.'

Slim leaned forward, but it didn't seem like anyone was planning to "have" him. The rustling was moving further away, the voices whispered, muffled. A commotion came from the hedgerow further up the road, something squeezing through branches. Two young people climbed down, ran across the road and disappeared into the woods on the other side. The taller of the two had worn greys and blacks, and a beanie hat had hidden much of his head from view, but the smaller person had been a girl with vividly dyed shoulder-length hair and a green parka Slim was sure he had seen somewhere before.

He walked across the road but they were long gone. He returned to the gate and climbed over. A short way inside the hedge, on a flat patch of ground, a couple of aerosol cans lay on a dirty blanket. A single condom packet in the grass at one end told him all he needed to know about the boy's intentions.

Teenagers, having a sniff then a tumble, if the boy had got his way. Slim wrinkled his nose, then picked up one of the cans. He turned it over, reading the small-print.

Non-toxic. Either the boy was sensitive to a bit of plain carbon, or as Slim thought more likely, he was an idiot.

And it said little for the girl who had chosen him as a companion.

Slim carried on up the hill until he reached the corner where Croad had climbed into the undergrowth to look for Dennis Sharp's old car. At least he thought it was the same corner, but as he pushed deeper and deeper into the woods, he saw no sign of it. By the time he stopped, certain he had walked far enough, he could no longer be sure which way he had come. With the undergrowth thinner heading downslope, he decided to continue on rather than climb back up to the road, curious as to where he would emerge.

Soon he was so deep into the woods that he could no longer even hear the distant rumble of an occasional car engine. The forest had flattened out, the undergrowth thinner, allowing him to move quickly, keeping the sun's occasional glimmer to one side to act as a rough direction marker.

From up ahead came the sound of water, and Slim stepped out of the trees to find himself beside a quiet stream trickling down through the woods. On the other side, the ground began to rise again. Further up the slope, the trees gave way to the overgrown corner of a field. The remains of a wire fence lay among brambles, its long-ago broken posts lying like unnaturally angular branches as they rotted amongst the rest of the fallen tree limbs.

Halfway to the crest of the hill, the stooped figure of a man was dragging something through the grass, down towards the trees.

Slim instinctively squatted low, easing himself down into a thicket from where he had cover but could still observe. His old military senses told him to perceive this newcomer as a threat.

The man wore a grey jacket over a white overall, and a baseball cap turned inside out. Wellington boots squelched through the field's boggy corner, white gloves holding on to something wrapped in clear plastic that Slim couldn't at first identify.

He shuffled closer, squinting through the undergrowth.

The skinned corpse of an animal. By its size and shape, most likely a young sheep.

The man's eyes darted back and forth as he dragged the corpse towards the river. Several times he stopped, crouched low and peered back over his shoulder as though anticipating pursuit.

A tramp? A stolen carcass he perhaps meant to cook or even sell on a local black-market? Slim crept closer, wanting to remember the face should he see it again.

The man was around Slim's age, mid-forties, clean shaven, his skin without blemish.

He didn't look like a tramp.

He reached the stream and began to pull the carcass upriver. Slim crept after him, wondering whether to reveal himself. Then the man slipped, his jacket catching on a twig as he stumbled, lifting long enough to reveal a logo printed on the overalls hidden beneath.

Slim froze.

Vincent's.

The man had come from the abattoir, but was concealing his identity. He had to be sneaking out from work or he wouldn't be wearing the uniform under his coat.

Slim continued his pursuit. A little further along, a mound of earth rose from the ground, the stream undercutting it. The man stepped into the water, hauling the carcass with him. He hefted it in his arms, tossing it ungainly back into a hollow carved out of the soft earth where the stream had created an undercut.

The man stepped back, nodded to himself, then climbed out of the river, and this time headed straight up the slope through the trees. Just before the woods gave way to the field, he pulled off the cap and turned it right way out, then slipped off the coat, rolled it up and tucked it under his overalls.

Slim watched the man until he had gone, then approached the undercut stream bank.

He stared.

The glint of other bags, partly covered with earth, came from underneath. Slim reached up and touched one. From the way the grain of the earth on the plastic felt under his fingers, he could tell it had been there for some time, months, possibly even years.

Slim, climbing up into the hollow, hauled one of the lower bags out until a glimmer of sunlight caught on the plastic.

Fearing what he might find, he pressed down until he saw the outline of what lay inside.

Not human, thank god. The putrid, rotting flesh of a sheep's foreleg.

Slim pushed it back into the hollow and stepped

back across the stream, quickly retracing his steps until the hollow was out of sight.

He needed a drink.

What he had seen made no sense. Why would anyone steal sheep carcasses and leave them hidden until they rotted away? Was the man an opportunist, or an idiot?

His routes back were through the woods the way he had come or up through the field. He chose to follow the route the man had taken, climbing up the steep field slope until the back of a squat, grey warehouse came into view.

Slim paused, staying close to the hedgerow.

Vincent's.

He found himself drawn to the place. Not just because the elusive Ellie worked there, or because of the mysterious hider of sheep carcasses, or even because of the hellhole of suffering and death it contained.

But because it sat like a central hub around which this mysterious community and its secrets revolved.

15

'So this is him?'

Slim flicked through the handful of photographs he had taken from the envelope Croad had brought. Some were grainy scans from newspaper cuttings, others were copies from group photographs. One was a clear portrait picture and a few others were snapshots of various angles of a forestry man at work.

Dennis Sharp had been fair-haired, bearded, tall and muscular. Attractive but for a slight sloping of the eyebrows which made him look suspicious. Even in school photographs he didn't smile, but there was no malice to his expression, only a guarded skepticism.

'Yeah, that's him. What I could find.' Croad grinned. 'Seen him wandering about the village? Perhaps wearing fake glasses and a wig?'

Slim was starting to tire of Croad's reluctance to offer much assistance, but the man was his only way into the background of Ozgood's life, so he just smiled.

'Not yet, but I'm still looking.'

'Not long til that next deadline. Mr. Ozgood wants this cleared up by then, you know that.'

'Mr. Ozgood has a lot more faith in my ability than I have, considering how little I have to go on.'

'I gave you that list.'

'I'm working through it. Three of the people on that list no longer live in the area. Three others told me they'd met Sharp no more than once or twice. And two of them are dead.'

Croad shrugged. 'My directory's out of date.'

'The person I'd most like to speak to is Ellie Ozgood, but she's off-limits.'

Croad shifted. 'Mr. Ozgood said—'

Slim lifted a hand. 'It doesn't have to be with your blessing. Tell me how she gets home from Vincent's and say nothing more about it.'

Croad winced, revealing his crooked line of teeth. Glancing around as though looking for the bugs he thought were still in place, he said, 'Stay away from her or I'll sort you before Ozgood ever gets near.'

Slim opened his mouth to respond but Croad had turned away, leaning over a work surface. His shoulders moved and then he was gone, out into the hall and through the front door without another word.

Slim looked down at the work surface. A small chalk board for reminders sat by an empty phone socket. Croad had scrawled "taxi, 5.35pm" in blue chalk.

Slim gave a slow nod, and then wiped the words away with a corner of his shirt.

16

NEITHER THE SHOP OWNER CATHY NOR THE BOY looked pleased to see him, but Slim gave them a cheerful smile as he set a can of spaghetti down on the counter.

'A shame half term is just a week,' he said. 'It must be nice having extra help around.'

Cathy flapped a hand at the boy. 'Nathan does nothing. Just sits around here causing trouble.'

'That's a shame. I guess you don't have the business here to need someone full time.'

Cathy lifted an eyebrow. 'Why, are you looking?'

'No.'

'A shame, because I could probably find some use for you.'

'Don't flirt with him, Mum,' Nathan said. 'Dad won't like it.'

Cathy clipped him around the ear. 'Watch your language. I wasn't flirting with him.'

'Yeah, you were. Think I'm stupid?'

Cathy scowled. 'You're half your father. Answer that yourself.'

'I'm telling Dad.'

'Think he'd care?'

'Give it a rest, won't you?'

This new voice came from an older girl. Slim looked up as she pushed through the curtain. He immediately recognised her, even though he had only seen her from behind as she fled through the trees. Plump around the waist, she wore her hair in three colours—a main dish of light brown bookended with curtains of rooty blond and speckled with highlights of pink that made Slim think of a cat with glitter caught in its fur. She looked Slim up and down with watery eyes out of a face too made-up to offer an idea of its base attractiveness, and smiled.

'You ain't from round here.'

Slim returned her smile. 'You're an astute one.'

'Name's Mandy,' the girl said, adopting a pout that left Slim expecting her to raise a smartphone in the air and click off a quick selfie.

'Do you go to the local school?' Slim said.

'What? I ain't that young. College. Study fashion design.'

'You have an eye for it,' Slim said, trying to sound sincere.

The girl pouted again. 'Thanks. Could give you a makeover if you like.'

'I appreciate the offer but I'm good with sweaters and jeans,' Slim said. 'And any colour other than black makes me look more cheerful than I am.'

The girl's reaction was masked by the mother stepping forward. 'So, just this then?' She held up the can of spaghetti, shaking it for emphasis.

Slim nodded. 'Though is there any chance I might speak to your husband? I'm something of a fan of local history, and I heard he was a good man to talk to.'

'Who told you that?' Cathy asked as the two children sniggered.

'Oh, a man I met in the pub.'

'I bet it was Thomas,' the girl said.

'Thomas?' Slim asked.

'Old Croad. Seen these two hanging around, my mate has. You're the one looking for Den, aren't you?'

Slim nodded. 'That's right.'

'No one told you yet he's dead?' The girl winked. 'If you like, I'll show you were he got smacked up. Bit dark up there. You'll have to hold me hand.'

This time it was the girl who took a clip round the ear. 'You two get back there,' Cathy said. 'And you, sir, should leave. We're past closing.'

Slim nodded. Arguing, the two kids went back through the curtain. The mother folded her arms in defiance.

'Not sure what you heard, but my husband knows little of what goes on outside a pint glass,' she said. 'And you want to watch yourself with old Thomas Croad. He's in Mr. Ozgood's pocket and that's not a place I'd wish on anyone.'

'I'll be careful.'

'You should. There's some that say Den's death

69

wasn't an accident, but that's not something you'd hear from me. Understand?'

Slim smiled, paid up and left. His attempt to get a contact inside Vincent's had failed, but as he turned a corner outside the shop he saw another chance. The girl, Mandy, was leaning up against a stone wall, one foot lifted behind her. Except for a light jacket she looked the same. Slim hesitated, but he had picked his path; he had no choice but to pass her or make an abrupt U-turn that would make his attempt to avoid her known.

'So is it true you've got money for Dennis Sharp's family?' Mandy said, stepping forward. She fiddled in her pocket as she looked up at him, withdrawing a packet of cigarettes. 'You smoke?'

'No.'

Mandy shrugged, lighting up. 'Don't tell me Mum.'

'She'd be angry?'

'She'd steal them. So what is it with Dennis Sharp? How much money?'

Slim held her gaze. The rumour he had planted had made its rounds. He saw an opportunity to plant another.

'There's no money,' he said. 'I'm a private investigator. I heard a rumour Dennis Sharp was still alive. I'm investigating an insurance fraud. He had a life insurance policy which paid out. If it's true he's alive then he's looking at a decent prison term.' He smiled. 'And I'm looking at a solid payday.'

Mandy shook her head. 'No, you're wasting your

time. Den's definitely dead. Went to his funeral, just to make sure.'

'What do you mean?'

She patted her stomach, and Slim realised that what he had assumed was an indulgence belly was in fact a slight bulge suggesting pregnancy.

'You don't know anything, do you?'

'About what?'

Mandy suddenly pouted and tossed her cigarette aside. 'Trying to stop, you know? I'm not really taking it all down. Just getting a little taste. Gonna be a good mummy, me.'

'You're pregnant?'

Mandy shrugged, pouting again. 'Yeah. Missed your chance, didn't you? Don't tell me Mum.'

Slim couldn't help but smile. 'We're not yet on first name terms so I'm sure that won't be a problem. What does your baby have to do with Dennis Sharp?'

'Nothing.'

Slim suppressed a sigh.

'Just glad he won't get her, that's all.' Mandy smiled. 'Definitely a girl, I just know it.'

'Get her?'

'Yeah. I mean, they never caught him, but we all knew he did it.'

Despite the cold, Slim felt a trickle of sweat run down his neck. 'Did what?'

'Killed them two kids.'

17

SLIM STARED AT THE PUB ACROSS THE ROAD, SET BACK behind its own car park and surrounded by a neatly manicured lawn. Two empty picnic tables stood outside. The car park was empty, but a single pint glass sat uncollected on the right-side table.

It was calling him.

Why hadn't Croad said anything about two dead kids? Mandy hadn't had time to elaborate, her mother calling her in. Slim hadn't wanted to show too much interest, but it had occupied his thoughts all night. Now, with grey dawn creeping over the village, he sat alone on a bench on the edge of the unkempt village green, wondering if he ought to start walking away before the pub opened.

From his position, Scuttleworth's single through-street angled by on his left, meandering past the church and the two shops, disappearing into farmland before it skirted Vincent's. A man was standing outside a house, sweeping. A lone crow cawed from atop the pub roof.

Slim's phone buzzed. He lifted the old Nokia to his ear. 'Don? Yeah, up early, guess it's a habit. You too, I suppose. Thanks for getting back to me, I really appreciate it.'

On the other end of the line, Donald Lane said, 'Still got nothing yet on that abattoir, but the two kids, that's an easy one.'

'Go on.'

'Was a while back. Oh five. House fire. It made the local BBC news for a day or two. Two kids left at home, eight and nine. Mother was out shopping instead of watching them.'

'Where?'

'I'm looking at a map of Scuttleworth now. Would have been on the road midway between the town and the abattoir. Got torn down.'

'Arson?'

'Place was an old leasehold, wiring found not to meet safety standards. The landlord got prosecuted, fined, made hefty payouts to both families.'

'The landlord?'

'Michael Ozgood. Oliver's father. Died in 2006, leaving the estate and businesses to his only son.'

Slim whistled through his teeth. There was worse to come; he could sense it.

'And these kids … who were they?'

'The oldest boy was Colin Kent, son of a local builder.'

Slim nodded. He remembered seeing Kent & Sons on a sign outside the local builder's merchant.

'And the other?'

A pause. 'You ready for this, Slim?'

'Hit me with it.'

'Steven Sharp. Aged eight. Dennis Sharp's younger half-brother.'

'I need a drink.'

'I thought you might. Hold on a minute. I'm not done.'

'I heard a rumour Dennis Sharp was involved.'

'Not exactly. He was working on a neigbouring property, building a stone wall. In the inquest, his mother, Shelly Holland, claimed she had told him she was going out, that he had promised to watch them. Dennis backed up her claim. As the crow flew, he was less than two hundred metres away. He could have heard the kids if one of them shouted, and he definitely should have heard the fire or seen the smoke. Yet by the time he made it back there, the house was an inferno, the two boys trapped inside, already long dead.'

Slim rubbed his eyebrow. 'Wow. That's suspicious as hell. Was there an investigation?'

'Yes. Dennis Sharp was considered a suspect, but the faulty wiring claim held up. The bodies of the two boys were found in the loft, where they had apparently been playing. Trapped by the smoke and fearing the fire downstairs, they tried to get out through a skylight that had rusted shut, according to the police report. Both suffocated from smoke inhalation. That was given as the cause of death. Of course their bodies were burned badly too, making identification difficult. Colin Kent was identified by dental records. Steve Sharp by a pendant he wore round his neck.'

Slim frowned. 'But not by dental records.'

Don sighed. 'He had no such record, as far as I could find out. I'm guessing that leaving the boys alone wasn't the only sign of motherly neglect.'

Slim nodded. 'Thanks, Don.'

'All good. I'll fax you the information if you can get me a number.' A chuckle. 'Where should I send the invoice? The usual place? Slim at sweet oblivion dot com?'

Slim laughed. 'Yeah, that would do. I owe you, Don.'

A chuckle. 'As always. Speak to you soon, Slim.'

As soon as he hung up the call, Slim leaned forward, head in his hands. It was happening all over again.

The time to back out was gone. The noose of curiosity had looped itself around his neck, and for better or worse, it was drawing tight.

18

To the northeast, the road clung to the brow of the hill, angling out of sight as it passed the flat roof of Vincent's, just visible above a line of trees. Before the road passed the abattoir, however, it dipped into a nearly invisible bowl, before rising again on the other side. A mechanics yard sat at the bottom of the shallow hill, lines of junked cars framing the road on either side.

In one corner was the plot where Dennis Sharp's family had lived, now replaced by a steel framed garage.

Slim watched a tendril of smoke rising into the air and listened to the distant thud of a hammer. The smoke rose from a small metal rubbish bin in one corner of the yard, while behind the hammering came the faint crackle of a radio voice broken by musical jingles.

Slim glanced behind him. The gateway where he stood shared a hedge with the adjoining property, a holiday let where Dennis Sharp had supposedly been working that day.

Don had followed up with a fax Slim had arranged at a post office in Harton, the next village to Scuttleworth's east. The two-hour roundtrip walk had been worth it to avoid Croad's involvement, but on the return journey, instead of heading straight back to the cottage, Slim had walked up through Scuttleworth to test out a theory.

The long-term holiday let had been unoccupied at the time of the fire. Slim had asked Don to check the weather on that day, and blue skies should have left the fire's smoke as visible as a firework display. Standing here by the gate, Slim could confirm any shouts from the boys or even the fire itself would have been easily audible.

Yet Dennis Sharp had done nothing.

On a follow-up call, Don had provided Slim with further details. Dennis's excuse: he had been wearing headphones, as he supposedly often did as he worked. And a single reliable witness had backed up his claim, an upstanding pillar of the community.

Ollie Ozgood.

19

SLIM RUBBED HIS TEMPLES AS HE SAT AT THE KITCHEN table, staring at his scrawled notes. A note pinned to the door had informed him that Croad was coming over just after lunch, leaving Slim barely an hour to collect his thoughts and then hide them before Ozgood's henchman showed up.

Stay focused, Slim tried to remind himself. He was being paid to discover if Dennis Sharp was still alive, but his investigation was leading him towards alternative reasons why he might have died.

Was it really true that Ozgood would have killed a man, risking his own future over a supposed rape even his daughter claimed was consensual? According to Croad's notes, Dennis Sharp had been thirty-eight at the time of his alleged crime, Ellie Ozgood sixteen. By British law, her age made Ellie legally an adult. It wasn't usual, but not impossible for a girl of her age to be involved with a man of his. Had killing him been necessary? A roughing up and a running out of town might have been more realistic.

Now, though, there was a case for an alibi. What if Dennis Sharp had been in some way involved in the deaths of the two boys? If Ozgood had used his standing in the community to push an alibi, it was clear that Dennis Sharp owed his boss a debt.

Had there been another reason for his murder that Ozgood was keeping quiet?

The sound of Croad's old Marina made Slim sit up. He gathered his papers together, put them into a plastic file, and slid the whole thing into a narrow space behind the fridge.

Croad was wearing an old QPR shirt which looked like it had been dragged through a forest. The team crest was still visible, but the sponsor's logo was a churned, stained mess.

'Wore this me first friendly with the first eleven,' Croad said, noticing Slim's look. 'Came on as a sub at seventy minutes. Put through this pass from mid which the lad up front hit against the woodwork. We went down two one.'

Slim smiled. 'What's on today's schedule?'

'Got a place you ought to see,' Croad said. 'Let's go. Engine's still running.'

Whether Croad was stalling to see if Slim would talk or just felt like he should be involved, Slim didn't know, but a drive out to the duel carriageway overpass where Dennis Sharp's message had requested the money be left seemed to serve no great purpose.

Slim leaned on a metal railing beside Croad,

watching the cars rushing by on the way to and from the Southwest. From here, of Ozgood's estate only the manor house to the north and a farm due northeast were visible. Scuttleworth was hidden by trees, as was Vincent's, but the uppermost point of the church spire just appeared out of the valley's dip.

'Right here, bang in the middle, ninth pole along,' Croad said, kicking the nearest barrier support for emphasis. 'In a black leather bag tied so it hangs over the carriageway, out of sight of the bridge road. One million quid in cash, two weeks from now. He's having a laugh, right?'

Slim nodded. 'Ozgood has no intention of paying up?'

'None. He's not even coming back until that afternoon, and he's only doing that to see if Den shows up.'

'Where is he now?'

'France. On business. He doesn't like getting his hands dirty, but I think for Den he'd make an exception. Found him yet?'

'I'm still working on the assumption that it's stolen identity. But let's say it is Den. What kind of man was he?'

'I told you before. Tough but decent, always had a smile and a joke but you know, he would wrestle a tree out of the ground.'

'That's not a lot to go on. I'm trying to get inside his personality.'

'That what you coppers call investigating, is it?'

'I'm not a copper, but yeah, it can help. Did he like music, art? TV? What kind of stuff would he watch?'

Croad scoffed. 'Didn't have one, what I saw only time I went round his house. And he wasn't one for much else. Didn't see no books, nothing like that.'

And no music, by association? Slim wanted to ask the question but Croad was still staring off into the distance, pretend chewing, considering something.

'He liked building these models,' Croad said at last.

'What, like Airfix, plastic planes, something like that?'

'Nah, from scratch. Little people made out of wire and twigs. Put them in poses, sat them on his window sills. Gave them braids made out of corn, like they was Afros or something, or dresses made from leaves. Little ballerinas. I remember he lamped someone in the pub what called him a poof, this guy who'd gone over to pick up an old sink Den was offloading, and had a look around. Was only joking but Den nailed him. You didn't mess with Den. Man who climbs trees and lugs rocks for a living ain't a guy you take on in the boozer even after a skinful.'

Slim nodded. 'Sounds like a tough guy with a sensitive side.'

Croad laughed. 'Yeah, all like that, ain't we?'

Slim said nothing. He let the silence fall between them, then, as he had hoped, Croad felt the need to fill it.

'Think he gave them to his kid brother, the one what died.'

'He had a brother who died?' Slim feigned surprise. 'You never mentioned him.'

'Not really important, was it? Died in a fire, what, oh four or five? I forget now.'

Slim didn't correct him. 'What happened?' he said.

'Don't know much except what the cops said. Kid and his mate playing at Den's mum's place. Wiring was bad. Was one of Mr. Ozgood's properties. Den was supposed to be watching the kids from the next property over while he was doing some maintenance work, but he went into town or something. Mr. Ozgood covered for him. Everyone was proper suspicious, saying Den did those kids in, but Mr. Ozgood got him out of that fire. Came out that the wires was bad and Old Mr. Ozgood got dinged. Ruined his reputation. Some said that did for him. Mr. Ozgood wasn't having any of that fall on him, though. He had his old man cough up to have every property put through proper safety testing. Cost him a packet I imagine.'

Slim just nodded. Separating the elements of truth in Croad's words from what felt like blind loyalty to his boss would take some doing. The old man was giving up more than he ever had before, even if Slim was no closer to figuring out what was going on.

'Where's all this leading?' Croad said at last.

Slim sighed. 'Way I can figure it, on the surface it doesn't look like there's any reason why Dennis Sharp— living or dead—would have any reason to blackmail Ozgood other than as a comeback against his own murder, which makes no sense, does it?'

'Why not?'

'Because if he was dead, he'd have nothing to complain about, and if he wasn't….' Slim trailed off, unsure where his train of thought was leading.

Croad's hand fell on Slim's shoulder. Wiry fingers squeezed flesh, and while there was nothing in Croad's strength that Slim couldn't have thrown off, there was a latent threat he found alarming.

'Just remember who's paying you,' Croad said. 'Find out if Den Sharp is alive, and if not, who's sending the threats. Don't concern yourself with anything else. What's past is past.'

20

CLORA BUZZED HIM INSIDE AS SHE HAD DONE ON HIS first visit. At the top of the stairs, he found she had made a vague attempt to clean up, with passageways cleared through the junk leading into the kitchen and back through into the living room, where Clora sat, as she had before, in an armchair facing the nearly concealed TV.

'Slim, isn't it?' she said, gesturing for him to sit down. Almost as soon as he'd cleared a space she made a repeated request for tea. 'You'll have to boil the kettle,' she added. 'You're in luck, though. Got a gap in my shows. Been meaning to get cable, but you know, I did get a box once, but down here in the valley I could never get the picture clear. Gave up in the end.'

'I could help you set one up if you like,' Slim said. 'I'm not much of a handyman, but I did a bit of electrics work back in the army.'

'Could you? That would be a love. Home help came

round the other day but they just move stuff about, you know. Don't listen to a word I say.'

'Home help?'

'Cos I'm on disability, see?' She shifted in the chair, her body rippling as though for emphasis. 'I can't get around like I used to and I can't manage those stairs. Dennis used to bring a box of stuff over from the shop once a week.' Clora smiled. 'That's how we got acquainted.'

Slim must have shown some surprise in his face, because Clora abruptly added, 'Oh, I never used to look like this. When you can't do nothing but eat and watch TV you end up in a vicious cycle. It's my hip. I bust it loading hog carcasses onto a lorry. He never did payout, that….' Clora trailed off, turning to glare at the host of some chat show as though she had been done a personal slight.

'I came to talk to you about Den,' Slim said. 'I know you were involved. I just wanted to know what he was like.'

Clora frowned. 'Why would you care? I thought you were looking for his relatives?'

Slim smiled. It would be better to tell her before the latest lies made their rounds. 'That wasn't entirely true. I am a private investigator, but I'm investigating a fraud claim. Specifically a rumour that Dennis Sharp might still be alive.'

Clora laughed. 'Oh, chance would be a fine thing. I'd welcome him with open arms.' She gave Slim a sly grin. 'And not just arms. As would a few other people.'

'I heard that he wasn't all that well liked.'

'Who told you that?'

Slim decided to keep his cards close for now, drawing out the information he sought one small piece at a time.

'A couple of guys I met in the village. I didn't take their names.'

'Young?'

'Uh, yeah.'

Clora rolled her eyes. 'Kids growing up on rumours. There was all that business with his brother and young Col, but that was years ago. That was all Ozgood's fault, anyway. He owns this place too,' she added, flapping a hand around her. 'Roof leaks. Tap in the bathroom trickles. How many times have I asked? He just sends old Croad around, who says he'll get someone out. Den would have been straight over with a bag of spanners.'

'I heard Ollie Ozgood provided Dennis with an alibi during the fire.'

Clora smiled. 'Ah, so you have heard? You P.I.s, always fishing for gossip.'

Slim felt himself blushing. It had been an uncharacteristic slip, but one he might be able to turn to his advantage.

'You got me,' he said. 'Just like the TV shows. I heard two kids died, the fire caused by faulty wiring. Also that Den was nearby, yet heard nothing. Ollie Ozgood claimed to have seen him, which was used as an alibi.'

Clora nodded. 'That's about as much as anyone knows.'

'Did you ever ask Den about it?'

86

'Yeah. He didn't like talking about it. Said it played out as the court heard. He wasn't close to Steve, but there was guilt there. You could see it. First time I asked him he stormed out. Didn't see him for a couple of weeks.'

'They weren't close in age, were they?'

Clora shook her head. 'Twenty odd years. Den had moved out before Steve came along.'

'I gather they had different fathers?'

Clora laughed. 'Safe to assume. Den told me once his mother had been a flower child in the sixties, all drugs and hippyish and that. Got knocked up at fifteen. Den never met his dad, just knew his name. It was just the two of them, until his mother started seeing Steve's dad. He didn't get on with Den, so Den moved out, started using his real dad's surname just to spite her. Next thing you know, she's pregnant by her new guy. I think Den felt she was replacing him.'

'Sounds like they had a complex relationship.'

'Oh, for sure. They were so close, but she was a bit of a loose cannon, you know what I mean? Unpredictable. No real surprise what happened to her. Steve was a tipping point, but that pushed her back to Den. Then, when he died, she fell over the edge. Have you seen her up there, camped over his grave?'

Slim nodded. 'I was introduced. It didn't go down well.'

'Her mind was fried long ago. A miracle her circuits held together so long.'

'What happened to Steve's dad?'

'Oh, Den told me he bailed a couple of years before

the fire. Him and her had a rough ride, so it was no surprise.'

Slim nodded slowly. 'It's a bit of a mess, really. So, tell me, what's your opinion on it all? About the kids, Den, and Ollie Ozgood providing an alibi?'

Clora frowned. 'Well, I'll tell you something. Old Ozgood was on his last legs when Steve and Col died. Ollie was set to take over soon. I mean, it probably hastened things by a year or two, but he was sick, about to go anyway, so people were saying.'

'So?'

'He didn't have the best of reputations. A tough man, tight with his money, hard on anyone who crossed him. That fire destroyed what was left of his reputation, but Ollie saw a chance to repair it by sticking his neck out for Den. Den was well liked, but a lot of suspicion fell on him after that fire. It wasn't pleasant. People breaking his windows, smashing up his car, that kind of thing. None of it to his face, of course, because Den was a man who could handle himself. But it was clear there were people about who wanted him out of the area.'

'So, by providing Den with an alibi, Ollie both protected Den's reputation and boosted his own?'

Clora nodded. 'I think that was the plan.'

Slim frowned. 'And did it work?'

'To an extent. Those who believed Den had their belief confirmed, while those who didn't only felt he was more involved, like Ollie was protecting him.'

'So it was a bit of a meaningless gesture?'

'It got the pigs off Den's back. Turned a bit of the hate back on Shelley, particularly from those who weren't sorry to her face. Bit of a nightmare all round, but like most things, it passed over after a while.' She shifted in her seat. 'What's all this matter anyway?'

Slim had noticed from his own phone that there was no reception down here in the valley, and Clora had no obvious electrical devices lying around. The grime on the door handle suggested few visitors, and Clora's own words suggested the Ozgoods had no place in her esteem. In a village of suspicious eyes Slim sensed an ally.

'It's a long story,' he said. 'How about I nip back to where I'm staying to pick a few things up, then tell you about it while I have a look at that leaking tap?'

21

WITH HIS ONLY ACTIVE TOUR OF DUTY BEING DURING the Gulf War, the jungle warfare skills Slim had learned in training had been mostly left on the shelf. Now as he approached Dennis Sharp's ruined house from through the trees to the rear, he applied some of the watchfulness that had been drilled into him during training exercises. Keep your body low, covered if possible. Move slowly, attuning to the sounds of the forest. Treat every unusual noise as a potential threat. Look out for anything reflecting the sunlight, any twig or branch not following a natural path.

It was extreme, but he neither wanted to alarm anyone who might be there nor leave a mark of his presence. He had no trust in Croad, to the point where he felt the old man had taken steps to hamper his investigation. So much was off limits, so much information inaccessible.

For a loner, the cottage seemed ideal. Set back from

a quiet road, it was entirely surrounded by forest, something which, in his paranoia, filled Slim with dread. Sharp, it seemed, had loved trees as much as people, meaning he had to have been happy here, even though the house was on Ozgood's land and the rent paid to his boss. Had Sharp felt an element of freedom here, or claustrophobia?

Slim reached the back wall and climbed over, an old pair of leather gloves keeping the brambles out of his face. What had once been a quaint garden of shrubs and flowerbeds fed by a sun that would only have been visible when directly overhead was now entirely reclaimed, a thicket of brambles broken only by a few hardy saplings shrugging off the thorny cloak as they pushed for the sky.

The back door had been broken off its hinges. Slim crouched in a corner of the garden by the wall, waiting some minutes before deciding it was safe to proceed. He had brought a digital camera so he took a few snaps, even making a short video. Then, holding it ahead of him, he approached the back of the house, moving through a dry animal track along the side wall.

He sat by the back door for a while, letting his eyes adjust to the gloom inside. He remembered something an old squad commander had told him about how eighteenth century pirates had worn an eyepatch not because they were missing an eye but to have one eye constantly adjusted to light and one to dark. With an ever present threat of attack, they could shift the patch back and forth as they entered or exited the gloomy hold into the bright sunlight on deck. Now, he kept one eye squeezed shut until he began to move forward.

Grime on the windows had left the inside of the house in perpetual gloom. Slim moved through one room at a time, clearing it out in a way he hadn't been able to during his visit with Croad, checking every sign of intrusion or habitation—foot marks in the dust, litter, bottles and cans, even the way the door handles felt beneath his palm—in order to ascertain when someone might have last been here. What was clear was that someone was regularly coming in and out.

Croad had admitted to doing so, and it was most likely that the caretaker of Ollie Ozgood's estate made regular rounds of the abandoned properties to check for squatters or other misuse. If there were secrets offering a clue to the blackmailer's identity, however, the property of the man being impersonated was a good place to start.

It was—or had been—a simple abode. A squat rectangle, the main entrance was in the centre at the front, the back door leading out of a utility room at the rear. The utility room led into a kitchen, the kitchen into a short hall with a living room on the left and a smaller bedroom on the right.

A one bedroom cottage with no cellar, and only a crawl space for a loft, there was nowhere obvious where a forgotten clue might be found.

Slim went out the front, sat down by the wall beside the front gate, and—no longer bothering to hide himself—opened his bag.

It had been wishful thinking that he might find some

hidden cupboard or secret room containing all Den's secrets. Nevertheless, despite the concrete floors and the stone walls, Slim had gone around tapping on the surfaces, more from paranoia than real hope. The detective he had slowly become over the years had longed for some secreted box of letters or photographs, but had come away disappointed.

The house was just as it appeared: an abandoned house.

He took a drink from a flask of coffee—wishing it were something far stronger—and then unfolded the map Croad had given him. The road led uphill, dropped into an adjacent valley, cutting through a ford then curving around to the right before passing the access road to Ozgood Hall.

Slim stood up. According to Croad, Dennis Sharp had been initially employed as a gardener, slowly gaining more duties until he was in charge of general maintenance across the whole estate. His main duty had been to maintain the gardens, however.

It made sense to assume Dennis Sharp was still alive. The how of it was not something that needed considering, but if he was, it helped to get into the man's mind.

Slim hoisted his bag and set off, retracing the route Den would have taken to work each day, hoping there might be some clue lying along the way.

22

THE CLOCKS HAD GONE BACK A COUPLE OF DAYS before. By the time Slim reached the access road to Ozgood Hall he was walking in darkness, the overhanging trees cutting off whatever twilight might have existed. Lights through the trees upslope indicated the hall, but the way they flickered as he walked made Slim nervous. There was something ominous about the house, something that made him feel uncomfortable.

He was almost happy to hear a car engine behind him as someone came thundering up the access road.

Slim was wearing black and had no light to warn them of his presence. He climbed off the road, stepping back into the trees. From his vantage point he peered out to watch the vehicle speed by.

A taxi from a local firm. In the back, the silhouette of a woman.

As the vehicle sped on, Slim stepped out and followed it at a jog, reaching the parking area outside

Ozgood Hall just as the taxi pulled up in front of the main doors.

An open area of lawn surrounded the parking area, offering little cover. As the driver climbed out to open the back door, Slim took his chance to sprint across the open space and duck down behind a raised flowerbed creating a neat semi-circle in front of the building.

Pushing a briefcase in front of her, Ellie Ozgood got out. The house lights gave Slim a clear view of a young woman dressed in a business suit, hair tied back, plain but not unattractive, a tired look about her. Then she was gone, up the steps into the hall.

Slim retained his vantage point until the taxi had gone. He was about to head back to the trees when the main doors opened again.

This time it was Croad who stepped out, the old man wearing a suit that looked horribly wrong on him, like an activist dressed in furs, a model decked out in an oily boiler suit. He walked to the bottom of the steps then just stood, looking out across the grounds, peering into the darkness.

After a couple of minutes he turned and went back inside, leaving Slim with the distinct impression that Croad had been waiting for him.

Or perhaps for someone else.

23

SLIM DIPPED THE SHEET OF PAPER INTO THE SINK THEN lifted it up. With a smile he tore it down the middle. The wet paper ripped unevenly, splitting apart in a jagged line. Slim stared at the pieces, feeling like he was looking at the two halves of his current investigation: the blackmailing of Ollie Ozgood, and Dennis Sharp's involvement in the death of his brother and a school friend.

He laid the two pieces down, the jagged edges roughly fitting together.

They had to be linked; it was impossible that they couldn't be. Yet one he was being paid to investigate, the other he was being warned off.

His moral compass had always swung wildly out of control, but he found it drawn to the children's cause more than Ollie Ozgood's. Slim had always favoured the oppressed over the oppressor, the underdog over the champion. He had never known what it had been like to be a father—his ex-wife had aborted their child when she took up with a butcher called Mr. Stiles—but he wondered how those left behind had dealt with their children's deaths.

Shelley Holland, it seemed, had dealt with her bereavement by having a complete breakdown, but what of the family of the other boy who died in the fire?

So, on a cold, drizzly Wednesday morning Slim found himself standing outside the gate of Kent & Sons, Construction Specialists.

It was a risk, he knew. Ollie Ozgood might be out of the country, but it wouldn't be good if Croad found out about his line of questioning. His protection was that Croad didn't seem much liked, and if it did get back that Slim was asking around about two boys dead for fifteen years, he could use an attempt to character profile Dennis Sharp as his excuse.

And if Croad didn't go for it?

Slim would worry about that when it came.

Inside the gate, a chained Labrador gave him a single lazy bark then went back to nosing in the bushes behind its kennel. Slim approached a prefab hut standing outside a main garage where two old trucks and a nicer four-wheel-drive land cruiser sat parked. A light was on in the hut, the hissing of a boiling kettle coming through an open window.

The door opened before Slim could reach it and a large, grizzled man leaned out, giving him a warm smile.

'I saw you come through the gate,' the man said.

'Got a brew going. Come inside and tell me how I can be of help for you today.'

The man had a habit of smacking his lips as though he'd just bitten into something juicy. Tattoos covered muscular forearms, and his hand as Slim gave it a shake felt like rock covered with sandpaper.

'Kenny Kent,' he said. 'I'm the *de facto* bloke in charge. My old man doesn't get out and about much these days.' He craned forward, peering sideways into Slim's face. 'What is it you're after? We can renovate or build from scratch. Or is it fencing you're after? We deal both with private and commercial properties.'

'Something else,' Slim said. He turned away, his eyes scanning the posters attached to the walls: adverts for construction vehicles, lists of rates, a couple of handwritten commendations from presumably minor local celebrities, and a large picture of a girl in a bikini advertising beer. The cabin had all the ingredients Slim had expected of a construction company—desks laden with untidy paperwork, a couple of hard hats lying in a corner, even a spirit level poking out of a bag grimy with cement dust.

'My name is John Hardy, but people call me Slim. I'm looking for a man called Dennis Sharp. I've been asking around the village with little success. I was walking by and thought I'd stop in on the off chance someone here knew him.'

He didn't look back. He waited, wondering if Kent would jump him, perhaps beat him to death. Out of the corner of his eye he saw Kent's reflection in a side window, translucent against a rusty fence outside. Kent stood still, staring at Slim's back.

'Well,' Kent said at last, letting out a breath that sounded as though he'd been holding it for several minutes. 'Even if he was alive, you wouldn't find that bastard round here.'

Slim turned. Kent was staring at a desktop, rubbing one eye with his fingertips.

'I heard what happened to your son. I know it was a long time ago, but I'm sorry. I can't imagine how hard it must have been.'

Kent frowned. He scratched a bald spot on the back of his head. 'Who are you? What did you have to come round here dragging that up for? I should throw you back out the door.'

'Please don't. I'm sorry if I've caused you distress, but I'm investigating a fraud claim possibly involving a faked death. Dennis Sharp might be alive, and if so, I need to find him. This may seem terribly intrusive, but I'm canvassing the area to see if anyone knows anything.'

Kent was staring straight ahead, looking through Slim at the wall behind, his eyes glazed over.

'I'm afraid, Slim, that he's dead and gone, and any claim you're investigating must be mistaken.' Kent's head moved slightly and his eyes met Slim's. 'But, if that bastard dared to come back to life, I'd send him back to hell again myself.'

24

Kent came back with two coffees, thick and black the way Slim liked it.

'I doubt there's anything I can tell you that you've not already heard,' Kent said, settling into his chair with a creak of leather. Slim had to make do with a metal fold-out, and he leaned forward to concentrate, praying Kent hadn't gone and laced the coffee as it tasted like he had. He was feeling that little tingle in his hands and face, the one he had once loved so much but had come to haunt him.

'Tell me anyway,' Slim said. 'I'm not sure what to make of anything I've heard.'

'It's Ozgood, isn't it?'

'What?'

'Who's put you up to this?'

'I don't think—'

'You tell that prick when you see him that he doesn't own everything around here. This is my land.' Kent stood up with surprising force, turning to point out of the window behind him. 'Three times he's sent that dog messenger of his around to tell me to shift my fence. Nineteen bloody inches he thinks it overhangs. It sits on my land, and I have the deeds to prove it. No one owns the air, do they?'

Slim, unsure of the law concerning property, height, and building regulations, just nodded. 'I wasn't planning to tell him I'd spoken to you,' he said. 'My investigation isn't going the way I had expected and it's been taking me into territory I'd consider … sensitive.'

Kent sat down, but he wasn't done. He leaned forward across the desk and poked a finger at Slim's chest. 'Ozgood, he's part of the bloody one percent,' he snapped. 'Never done a day's work in his life yet his shadow hangs over Scuttleworth like some stinking cloud. You can't turn round without meeting one of his little parrots, one of his little yes-men out trying to squeeze an inch out of someone. You get me?'

Slim nodded. 'He hired me for this investigation, but I'm no one's parrot. If I'm honest with you, I took this job because I was desperate for work, barely one step above the street. I'm just trying to find out what's going on and if there are any truths to the claim. All the evidence points to Dennis Sharp being dead, but I need to confirm it. And in the event that he's somehow not, I need to build up a picture of the man in order to better understand him, and therefore anticipate his next move.'

'So what do you want me to tell you? That he was a fine member of the community and that he'd never do something like that?'

Slim was dismayed to find his coffee cup was empty. His hands had begun to shake so he put it down, then put his hands on his lap so Kent wouldn't see them shaking. Looking up again, he shook his head. 'No. I want you to tell me what you really think.'

'That evil bastard killed my son, and Ozgood covered for him. I wasn't sad when he ran off the road. Some say he was drunk, others that it was fixed. The pigs didn't look too hard, no one has any doubt of that. If anyone tells you otherwise, they're lying.'

'And what about Ellie Ozgood?'

'What about her?' Kent spat at a rubbish bin, the glob of phlegm catching on the lip and dripping inside. 'Self-entitled bitch.'

'Dennis got accused of rape.'

Kent waved a hand. 'A set up. Ozgood made a blunder giving Den an alibi. Might have been a few women round here who had their eye on him, but most folk knew he did it. Ozgood pulled that fake rape charge to try and change opinion. I don't know, maybe Den was getting old, time to move on.'

Slim's head was spinning. He heard Kent offer him another coffee and he nodded. Out of the corner of his eye he caught Kent taking an unlabeled bottle off a lower shelf and adding a little medicine.

As Kent returned, putting the fresh brew down in front of him, Slim said, 'So you have no doubt? Dennis Sharp killed your son?'

Kent punched the tabletop. 'None. The guy was rotten through and through. We all knew it even back in his school days. Weird kid, not surprising with that mother. Always warned my kids off letting him get too close. He was always out and about somewhere, you see. Never drove anywhere. Always walked. Never had a torch either. He'd appear right beside you out of the dark.'

Slim wanted to ask more but the door rattled as someone came in. Kent looked up, smiling.

'Jimmy. My boy. Lad, come here, say hello. This here's Slim. He's been asking round about Den Sharp.'

Slim turned. The young man was perhaps twenty, crewcut, hard-eyed. Thin but tightly muscled as though he helped out his dad.

Slim didn't recognise him until the young man spoke.

'What's he doing in here, Dad? Everyone's talking about him. Poking his nose in where it isn't wanted.'

Slim nodded. The voice he had heard from the gateway: the young man pushing an aerosol onto his unwilling girlfriend. An idiot trying to push his idiocy onto someone else.

'Jimmy,' Slim said, his voice slurring as he pushed himself uncertainly to his feet. 'I found something you left behind.'

'What?'

Slim was dimly aware that Jimmy's fists had clenched. He grinned. 'A couple of spray cans. Oh, and a condom. Unused.'

25

Slim stumbled back towards his lodgings, occasionally rubbing his left cheek, pressing down on the cut Jimmy's ring had opened until he was sure the blood had stopped.

It felt strange to have an enemy. He'd been here a few days without one readily presenting itself, but Jimmy had now ticked another box on Slim's case disaster sheet.

Kenny Kent's son had got off a decent left hook before his father grabbed him, bear arms pinning scrawny ones to the boy's side. The idiot boy had caught Slim flush on the cheek bone, but the ring had done the only real damage, Kent's son spending more time idling in fields with spray cans rather than carrying fence poles, judging by the lack of weight behind the blow.

The scuffle had rather severed Slim's conversation with Kenny Kent. He had made a hasty exit, getting out of sight while father argued with boy. He had intended to head straight back to his lodgings but had instead made a U-turn detour to buy a cheap bottle of brandy from Cathy's shop. Mandy, running the store in place of her mother, had asked him what had happened, but Slim had laughed about low-hanging tree branches and stumbled out.

Now, still not in sight of his lodgings, the brandy was gone and Slim was considering returning for more. Scuttleworth had been up the hill, hadn't it?

He decided to sit for a while and think about it, but when he lowered himself to the verge, he found no ground beneath him, and instead he rolled head over heels back into the undergrowth.

When he came to a stop he was no longer sure in which way the road lay, so he rested his head back and stared up at the nearly leafless tree branches overhead.

Was this a relapse or was he off the wagon again? Slim found he barely cared, only that the softly crunchy twigs and leaves beneath him felt strangely comforting, as though someone had laid a cool blanket down to cushion him.

The world was revolving faster and faster, the branches above becoming a kaleidoscopic blur. Slim tried to close his eyes but that only made it worse, the spinning seeming to begin with his head and engulf his whole body. He had the sensation of choking, of hot vomit filling his throat, and then he was rolling again, this time onto his front.

The trees disappeared. The ground beneath him was black. Slim smelt warm peaty earth. It soothed him, slowing the spinning sensation, and he thought that he slept.

~

The crunch of footfalls nearby was the first sound upon waking. Slim opened his eyes. His face ached and his body felt leaden. The spinning sensation had slowed but not stopped so he knew he was still drunk. He shifted a couple of inches until he could see rays of sunlight catching the ground in front of his face.

From the chill of his back beneath his jacket and the angle of the sun, he judged it to be late afternoon. He had been lying inert for several hours.

The footsteps came again, a distinct crunch of feet on fallen leaves and twigs. It had to be a person, most likely a man—no animal save a horse or cow would make such heavy footfalls.

Acutely aware that he could be in danger, Slim gently rolled over onto his side.

He had fallen into a shallow hollow behind a fallen branch. A bent elbow in the branch gave him a triangular viewpoint from which to observe the slope of the forest below as it angled down to the river.

A man was walking lower down. Moving slowly, he would move forward a few steps then squat, reach out for something, pick it and put it into a bag.

Slim glanced left and right. The grey head of a mushroom poked out of a bed of leaves just a few paces beyond the fallen branch.

He let out a slow breath. Just an autumn mushroom picker, not someone come to finish him off.

The man stood up. He wore a light brown camouflage jacket over grey jeans and a deerstalker hat. A tatty rucksack hung over one shoulder, and Slim watched as the man turned, slipping it off his arm and unzipping it to put a bag of grey-white mushrooms inside.

Slim's breath caught in his throat. The face angled up to the sun, giving Slim a view of the man in profile. A light brown beard was flecked with grey, and the face was more lined, but the eyes and the suspicious tilt of the man's brow made Slim wish his vision would stop wavering long enough to see this face in total clarity.

The clothes were a match, the beard, the angle of the jaw....

Slim had stared at this face every morning for the past week.

Dennis Sharp.

He shifted, trying to get up, but he was still too intoxicated to control himself. A twig snapped beneath his hip, the crack like a gunshot across the still of the forest.

In an instant Sharp was gone, dropping low and racing down through the trees. Slim scrambled to his feet, but by the time he got around the fallen branch, Dennis was long gone.

He cursed his foul luck, but at the same time felt a bloom of elation.

He knew it for certain now.

Dennis Sharp was alive.

26

'First threat came as both email and letter. Letter came first, then the email, a copy. Secretary had it filed with all the other junk Mr. Ozgood gets. Thought you might like to see it.'

Croad held out the sheet of paper. Slim took it and frowned. 'This is a photocopy.'

'Don't have authorisation to give you the original.'

Slim suppressed a sigh. 'This will be of limited use if you want it analysed. Has no one looked at it before?'

Croad shook his head. 'Mr. Ozgood doesn't want the police involved. You know that. They only know about the stuff that happened official, like Den's crash and Ellie's court case.'

'Well, I'll see what I can do. Can you find me something to compare it with?'

'Like what?'

'Something with Dennis Sharp's writing on it.'

Croad nodded. 'Will do me best.'

He went out. Slim slumped back to the table, hooking his feet together in an attempt to stop the shaking. It had been tough hiding his relapse from Croad, and the old man didn't appear to have heard about his run in with Jimmy Kent. In such a small community though, it was inevitable that sooner or later word would get around.

Neither had Slim mentioned the man in the forest. A day had gone by since then, during which Slim had holed himself up, fighting the urge to drown himself, and already the doubts were creeping in. Had he really seen Dennis Sharp, or just someone with an uncanny likeness? He had been in the middle of a sudden relapse after more than three weeks sober. Had he even seen anyone at all?

He had followed the man, but Den had done exactly what Slim would have done in the circumstances: run to the nearest stream then follow it to hide his trail. Slim had followed the stream until it reached a ford where he had given up. Backtracking, he had struggled to remember exactly where he had started and therefore failed to find any tracks.

He was beginning to doubt his own sanity.

Needing to keep his mind occupied, he went outside, walked up the hill a short distance until his phone caught a signal, then called Kay.

'How's the Ozgood investigation going?' his friend asked.

'I'm still alive,' Slim answered. 'I consider that a win so far. I have something I'd like you to look at.'

'Sure, you got a fax or is it something you need to post?'

Slim considered. Kay and himself had been loose friends over the years, but stuck in this unforgiving nowhere town, more than anything he wanted to see a familiar face.

'Any chance you could come down?'

A pause. Then Kay said, 'Sure. I can be there tonight.'

Slim arranged a meeting place in Stickwool, where he had met the police officer Evan Ford, then hung off. Next he called Croad.

'Have you found me anything?'

'Yeah. Bringing it back now.'

'I'm going out. Leave it in the postbox.'

As soon as he had hung up, Slim walked back down to the house, went inside and locked the front door. He then did the same to the back. He went into the bedroom, intending to climb into the bed and sleep, but at the last moment deciding instead to slide under the bed, out of sight.

Lying there in a dusty space barely high enough to fit him, he felt like an idiot, but he had only been there a couple of minutes when he heard someone rattling the door handle. Croad, it had to be.

A key turned in the lock and the door creaked as it opened. Footfalls fell on the lino in the entrance and then moved up the hall to the kitchen. Slim had left the bedroom door ajar and he watched a shadow pass by, heading into the kitchen.

Papers rustled as Croad looked through Slim's notes.

It was no surprise that the caretaker had a spare key, but Slim felt a rising anger that he was being spied on. He had left nothing incriminating where Croad could find it, but the cheek of the man was incredible.

Giving up or clearly not finding what he wanted, the shadow retreated to the door. It creaked open as Croad let himself out, then the key turned with a click.

Slim was breathing hard, his face sweaty despite the cold. He climbed out from beneath the bed and went to the kitchen. He looked through his papers but Croad had taken nothing.

He pulled out a chair and sat down. He was wondering whether a coffee might make him feel better when a distant bang followed by a growl announced the approach of a car.

Slim went through into the living room and cracked the curtain just as Croad parked his ancient Marina and got out. The old man stumped up to the door, pushed something through the letter box, and then retreated to the car without looking up, muttering something barely audible about being due a pay rise.

Slim stared as the car pulled away with an irritated whine.

His throat was dry, his temples throbbing. 'Leave me alone, you bastard,' he muttered to the ghost of Dennis Sharp. 'I don't need to be haunted.'

27

'I've seen him,' Slim said, leaning across the table. 'Twice.'

Kay Skelton frowned. Powerful fingers which defied the delicate forensic linguistics work in which he was now primarily involved made a steeple on the tabletop. He chewed silently, considering.

'You're sure?'

Slim shook his head. 'Am I ever sure of anything? No. The first time I was drunk. The second, I only know who it wasn't. I didn't see his face.'

Kay gave a sage nod. 'That doesn't mean you were mistaken. But I've known you long enough to know that the way you interpret things isn't always the same as the rest of us.'

A waitress brought coffee. Slim took a sip then called her back, asking for an extra shot of espresso. Kay watched Slim out of grey eyes as he slowly drank.

'You knew Ozgood in the military,' Slim said. 'What was he like?'

'You mean, was he a born killer or a made one?'

'Something like that.'

'You want my honest opinion?' Kay sighed. 'He was a coward. He didn't have the stomach for it. But something else ... his personality was—what's the easiest way to put it?—entitled. We all knew he was a rich kid. He knew it, too. He tried to be one of us—tried pretty hard—but it was like he came in a different wrapper. I mean, we all came from different backgrounds—my old man was a welder; Trey Phillips—remember him?—his dad was a banker—but Ozgood, he was on a different level. Like, we'd hit a bar on a down day and he'd want to set up a tab. Trying to be matey, buy us all drinks to get us on side, but he stumbled each time. We saw through it. Then, when we were on active duty fighting insurgents in Somalia, he damn sure made certain he was behind the radio rather than out in the ATVs.'

'Didn't you ever see him kill a man?'

Kay shook his head. 'It would never have happened. Didn't have the guts. But one thing—'

'What?'

'Ollie had a temper. Petulant, like a child. Someone swapped out his boots for a size small one day, and he went off like a little kid, throwing stuff around. Went straight to the sergeant, filing a complaint. No one missed him when he signed off.'

Slim gave a slow nod. 'Could he have killed someone?'

Kay laughed then shook his head. 'I know what he

claimed, which I told you, but having known him, I find it hard to believe. Certainly not with his own hands. He could have ordered it—he was rich and angry enough—but he would have stayed well away, made sure not to get his hands dirty.'

Slim gave a thoughtful nod. Another theory was settling into place.

'This man Dennis Sharp is supposed to be dead. That's what Ozgood tells me. He set it up, he made sure of it. That's his trump card, what he told me with such conviction as though that should define him more than anything else. I've heard Dennis was loved and hated in equal measure, but what if it wasn't like that at all? What if his death was faked, or it never happened at all?'

Kay smiled. 'That's a lot of "what if's", Slim, and do you know who says that? A drinker. The detective needs to think about the "whats" and drop the "ifs".'

Slim nodded. 'That's one reason I called you.' He pulled a folder out of his bag and handed Kay several photocopies.

'This is the copy of the original blackmail letter. These are account ledgers for Ozgood's garden supplies. Dennis Sharp wrote these by hand. What I need to know is if the same person wrote both.'

'Couldn't you get the originals? I could do a lot more with those.'

Slim shook his head. 'Croad—Ozgood's caretaker—wouldn't give them to me. He said they were too valuable.'

Kay smirked. 'I can understand the letter, but those old gardening ledgers? Not so much.'

Slim shrugged. 'He's a strange one.'

Kay leaned over the papers. Slim offered him a pen which Kay took, frowning as he stared at the copies.

'It'll take me a few days to be certain,' he said, 'plus without the originals it'll make it difficult to assess things like indentation strength. However, I should be able to narrow it down to a maybe or a straight no.'

Slim nodded. Lined up side by side, the two texts looked nothing alike. The letter was bunched and scrawled, the lines uneven, the ledger neatly filled out in grammar school copperplate.

'I mean, he could have written it left-handed, or had someone else write it,' Slim said. 'Or done one of those newspaper print things.'

Kay looked up. 'That the blackmailer bothered to write a letter at all is something to consider,' Kay said. 'Who writes letters these days? They must have known it would be checked. If I could get the original I could check it for prints.'

'I'll ask Croad, but don't expect much,' Slim said.

Kay nodded. He slipped the papers into the bag and stood up. 'I'll be in touch. It was good to see you, Slim.'

They shook hands. Slim watched Kay walk out of the cafe, resisting a sudden urge to call his old friend back.

I'm afraid, he didn't say. *I don't want to face this alone.*

28

SCUTTLEWORTH'S COMMUNITY HALL WAS EASY TO overlook, sat as it was on a carved platform at the top of a field, and at the end of an easy to miss lane between two houses a few doors down from Cathy's shop. Slim, unwilling to talk with anyone, found himself pushing through a creaking pair of double fire doors into a pleasantly lit, high-ceilinged room. Frayed tape left tram lines for any number of indoor sports in a place large enough for a badminton court, while doors at the far end accessed other function rooms: a kitchen, small library, display rooms. Windows on one side looked onto the back fences of a row of houses, while those on the other side had a pleasant view of farmland sloping into a forested valley. Slim, frowned, remembering what he had seen down there in the woods. His fingers closed over the comforting coldness of the brandy bottle he had bought in Cathy's shop which he now carried around as a crutch, even though, by some miracle, he was yet to open it.

Slim wandered through into the kitchen, dropped a pound into an honesty box and helped himself to a strong cup of instant coffee. As the spoonfuls of grains piled up, he felt a pang of guilt and added an extra fifty pence.

A little terrace at the back accessed through a sliding door had a pair of plastic tables, with chairs in a stack by the door. Slim took his coffee and sat outside, pulling his jacket around him against a chill wind rushing up from the valley.

He took a sip of the coffee and found it nearly cold already. He knew how to heat it up in a way he would most like, but he resisted, keeping his fingers firmly pressed against the tabletop even as the chill set in. He watched a tractor driving around the edge of a field across the valley for a few minutes, the farmer occasionally jumping down to inspect sections of fence, then stood up and went back inside.

He washed the cup in a sink then wandered through into the adjacent library room. Partly a kids' play area, with a few boxes of toys in one corner, and partly a local history library, he thumbed absently through a volume of collected parish council meeting minutes. It was all the usual local stuff—requests for no-littering signs, debates over the implementation of speed bumps through the village, notices for lost pets, primary school charity events—the kind of comforting inanity of which Slim sometimes wished he could be part.

The list of attendees was an interesting snapshot of village life. Among some Slim didn't recognise were others he did: Cathy Jenkins, Kenny Kent, even Clora for a few months as he flicked through, serving as treasurer. The names came and went as Slim turned the pages—Cathy served a year as community hall secretary, disappeared for a year then returned as deputy head—revealing a fluctuating sphere of influence as people came, grew, faded, went.

Beneath the list of serving councillors was an addendum containing the names of those also in attendance.

Slim frowned at the sight of a familiar name. He flicked back through the minutes to the previous month, then again. Further back, month by month, even as the councillors came and went, the name was always there, a watcher in the crowd no matter how large or small, as though to influence proceedings by his very presence alone.

Thomas Croad.

29

CATHY'S SHOP SOLD LITTLE IN THE WAY OF READILY edible food, so Slim found himself sitting on a bench outside the church dipping slices of bread into a cold can of out-of-date baked beans. An open can of coke sat beside him, taunting him with the ease with which he could top it up with the goodness in his pocket.

The leaves had mostly gone from the trees, collecting in ditches in gummy, matted clumps. A herd of sheep in a neighbouring field were a continuing audible accompaniment, but otherwise Scuttleworth was at rest. A car had driven past ten minutes before, but since then Slim had felt like the only person alive in this forgotten place.

And then a plaintive cry broke the calm and Slim knew another confrontation was coming.

Shelly.

He finished his lunch, dropping the rubbish into a stone bin by the end of the path, and then made his way around the church to the rear graveyard. Now that he knew it was there, he could make out the awning of Shelly's tent through the trees.

The door flap was down but the sounds of someone shuffling around came from inside. Slim paused, reached into his pocket and pulled out the brandy. He unscrewed the top and took a swig.

The liquor's harsh burn sank into his muscles with immediate effect. Slim sighed then sat down on the path.

'Hey, Shelly,' he called. 'I'm the guy who showed up the other day with Croad. I've ditched that arsehole, so I was wondering if we could have a chat about your sons.' He paused. 'Both of them.'

The shuffling stopped, the tent going quiet. Slim took another drink as he waited.

'I know some people think Dennis killed those kids,' Slim said, staring off across the field. 'You know what I think?' He waved his free hand at nothing. 'I think Dennis is still alive, and I'm waiting for him to show up and tell me himself.'

The tent door billowed. Slim saw a shadow moving, something long and pale bending and curving.

The drinking had dulled his reactions over the years. He managed to close his eyes, but that was all as Shelly's scowling face appeared, her arm cocking and unleashing, sending a multi-limbed projectile flying straight into his face.

30

HE ONLY HAD SMALL CHANGE LEFT SO HE EMPTIED IT into the honesty box and took the coffee out to the terrace. This time he made no attempt to control himself, emptying a good third of the brandy's remaining contents into the cup.

He drank while holding a wad of toilet tissue to the cut on his cheek, wishing he'd stayed put. He lifted the object that had hit him and turned it over in his hands— a doll made from twigs and wire—thankful it hadn't been a rock or knife. He wiped a spot of his own blood off it then stuffed it into his pocket. Shelly had shown herself only for a moment before pulling the flap closed, shutting off their brief interaction almost as soon as it had begun.

When he was finished with his drink, he stumbled back inside the community hall, into the library, where he sat down again with the collection of old parish council notes. He wished he was sober enough to read, but his focus would only extend to pictures, so he found himself flicking over old black and white photographs of village fetes, seasonal festivals, local sports clubs, village outings.

Nothing except more questions. His head slumped towards the desk. He was beyond weary, in a place where the possibility existed to sleep forever. His fingers clawed at the paper, wishing it were a rope that would pull him out of this place.

The door clicked behind him. 'Excuse me. You're not allowed alcohol in here.'

Slim looked up, squinting to focus. A young girl stood in the doorway, her hair tied up with a floral patterned scrunchie. Blue eyes shone out of a pretty face which seemed to be surrounded by a purplish-pink aura.

It took him a moment to recognise Mandy.

'I don't have alcohol.'

'You do. I can smell it.'

'I already drank it.'

The girl gave him a sympathetic shrug. 'And I don't want it coming back up all over a bunch of books I can't replace. Even if you are the only person I've ever seen actually read them. Look, if you're cold, you can sit in the kitchen.'

'Do I look like a tramp?' Slim said.

'Well, kind of. Especially with your face. I might think it if I hadn't seen your money in me mum's shop.' She sighed. 'Look, come on. I'll make you a coffee.'

'I think I drank most of it already.'

'Well, you pretty much own it. You know how few people use that box?'

'It was just a bit of change.'

Mandy laughed. 'You must be hammered. You put in nearly eight quid.'

'Is that so? Well, if you're restocking, I can recommend a couple of decent brands.'

He stood up, his balance uncertain, but using door frames and the wall for support he followed Mandy out into the kitchen. She pulled a seat out for him then took one across the table.

'So what happened?' the girl asked as she waited for the kettle to boil. 'You look like you've had a rough couple of days.'

'What makes you say that?'

Mandy laughed. 'Nothing like a sense of humour. What happened to your cheek?'

'Which one?'

'Well, both I suppose.'

Slim pointed. 'This one was a punch from a guy wearing a ring. And this was from an old lady throwing a wooden doll.'

Mandy shrugged. 'Sounds like a usual day in Scuttleworth,' she said. 'I can't lay claim to the old lady, but it was my boyfriend who punched you. Well,'—she rolled her eyes—'as of this morning, ex-boyfriend.'

31

IN ADDITION TO SPORADICALLY ATTENDING A FASHION college in Exeter, among other things, Mandy was employed for a few hours a week as the community hall's cleaner.

'Pays better than me mum does,' she said as way of explanation. 'And even the hoover's less annoying than her constant whining.'

'So tell me,' Slim said, leaning against a countertop for balance while Mandy washed the cups in the sink. 'You seem like a nice girl. Everyone I've met round here has some issue or other, but the more time I spend with you, the more I think that you might actually be normal. Therefore, why were you hanging around with a muppet like Jimmy Kent?'

She shrugged, her back to him. 'He's all right when he's not off his head,' she said. Then, with a quick glance back, she added, 'and it's not like there's a lot of choice around here, is there?'

'Never heard of buses? Trains? You could get out of here. What about fashion college?'

Mandy laughed. 'They're all primas or poofs, aren't they? Anyway, Scuttleworth's where I grew up. You get used to it. You're full of questions, ain't you? So, my turn. Why do they call you Slim?'

Slim hesitated. 'It's a long story, but not an interesting one. It involves a pipe. I'll tell you when you're in a good mood, ruin your day.'

'Is that an offer?'

Slim shrugged. 'Maybe.'

'Wow. Next time something's going well I'll be sure to give you a call.'

'You do that. So, is it worth me asking you about Dennis Sharp?'

Mandy cocked her head. 'I told you. He was a perv. Killed those kids.'

'And you know that for sure, do you?'

Mandy pouted. 'Look. I didn't know him well. Not personally. Saw him around from time to time. I know he died in a car crash, but I was pretty young when it happened so I don't remember much about it. I remember going to his funeral with me parents, but only because he was local. Whenever someone local dies, everyone shows up. That's just the way it is.'

'Did you ever speak to him?'

'Dunno, don't think I ever did one-to-one. He did some craft stuff here from time to time, special occasions, that kind of thing. Kept himself to himself, mostly, what I remember.'

'And what did other people think of him?'

Mandy frowned. 'Look, is this something that'll come back around to bite me? You might get a bit of gossip out of some of the old dears who come in here on coffee mornings but I've told you enough tales already. Plus, you're hammered. Are you going to remember any of this?'

Sober, Slim might have kept his cards closer, but he had a way of thinking about a case which wouldn't reveal its secrets: break it open, stamp it, kick the nest. Loosen the lock holding it closed, create something out of nothing.

'I don't think he's dead,' Slim said. 'In fact, I know he's not. I saw him, walking in the forest.'

Mandy laughed. 'You're out of your mind. I mean, it's a cool story, but it's not very likely, is it?'

'I told you, I saw him.'

'Were you drunk?'

Slim grimaced. 'I'd had one or two.'

'So that's a yes. Look, Slim, I've enjoyed talking to you, but I have to get on and get this place cleaned, if you don't mind.'

32

SLIM WOKE TO THE BUZZING OF HIS PHONE. HE scrambled for it, finding it nestled into his armpit. He was lying on the sofa in the cottage's small living room, his body covered with a towel, his legs exposed to the chill November air. Sunlight pierced holes in the threadbare curtains as Slim sat up and began frantically massaging warmth back into his stiff, frozen limbs.

He didn't remember falling asleep, but the sunlight gave him hope. It was a new day, and a new beginning. A fresh start. The recovery mantra had been drummed into him at an addiction meeting an old criminal conviction had required him to attend as part of his sentence, but it had taken years to sink in. Now, he scraped the wreckage of yesterday's disaster into a plastic bag and brewed the kettle. Then he went to see who had called.

Kay. He tried to call back but just as the phone picked up a single bar of signal, the battery abruptly died. Slim found the cable and plugged it in, then went for a short walk outside while he waited for his phone to regain enough power for the call.

The woods were quiet. Barely even a whisper of a breeze rustled the leaves yet to fall from the trees or those piling in brittle mounds on the forest floor. Slim turned in a slow circle, wondering if Dennis Sharp were out there now, watching him, and if so, what he was thinking.

'I don't care if you get Ozgood's money,' Slim muttered to no one. 'You can have all of it as far as I care. Just show your face. Let me take a good look at you. Trust me, I know what it feels like to be disappeared.'

No answer came. Slim went back inside and found his phone had enough charge to make a call. Reception was poor, but by standing on a chair next to a window he was able to get just enough of a signal to call Kay back.

'It's me.'

'You don't sound good, Slim. Are you all right?'

Slim laughed. 'Hanging in there. Just eating a bowl of fresh fruit for breakfast.'

'Well, I have some news. It might cheer you up, we'll see.'

'What is it?'

'I did an analysis on the handwriting samples you gave me. Now, my professional opinion on this is only worth about eighty percent, but I think we have a match. They look different to the naked eye, but the letter contains certain depths of stroke and intensity that suggest it was the same person trying to disguise their handwriting, perhaps by holding the pen differently or by writing drunk.'

'How can you tell? They looked completely different.'

'A lot more writing comes from the shoulder than people realise. Then there's the balance of the letters. Like I say, I'm only eighty percent, but in this game that's decent. My guess is that whoever did it was pretty naive, new to this. You're dealing with an amateur, that's for certain. Now, if you could find me an actual text written by Dennis Sharp—a letter or article, for instance —I could do a syntax analysis which would add another layer of probability.'

'Syntax analysis?'

'People use certain repeat phrases that can be matched. An amateur blackmailer might have no idea what clues they're leaving in the words they use. Then there's tone, and the obvious one, spelling.'

'I'll see what I can get.'

'I look forward to it. Always glad to help. You hang in there, Slim.'

Kay hung up. Slim stared out into the forest.

Dennis Sharp was alive. He knew it.

33

'AND PUT THAT DESK OVER THERE,' CLORA SAID, waving a hand in the rough direction of a cleared space in the corner. 'I never use it so I might as well get it out of the way.'

Slim sweated as he hauled the heavy block of mahogany across the room, wondering both why Clora had it and how she had gotten it up the stairs.

'Phew,' she said as he set it down. 'It's tiring me out just watching you. I'm ready for another cuppa whenever you are.'

Slim grunted in place of a reply, wondering when his fitness had got so bad. However, clearing Clora's flat into even a semblance of order had been as hard as much of his army training. Fourteen full refuse sacks stood by the door. Slim had unearthed furniture Clora had forgotten even existed. She kept reminding him that he ought to be proud of his efforts, even though her own contribution had amounted to one solitary shift from the armchair to a recently rediscovered sofa in order to test a new angle of facing the TV.

'You ought to ask Ozgood for a job,' she said. 'You're far more use than that idiot Croad.'

'Thanks.'

'You look exhausted. You should take a rest. Didn't you sleep last night?'

'Barely.'

Clora laughed. 'I'd sleep forever if I didn't have my shows.'

'I don't really watch television,' Slim said. 'I owned one once, but it got busted.'

'You dropped it?'

He grimaced. 'House fire.'

'Oh.'

He made tea and coffee while Clora made herself comfortable.

'Now I can get to the piping cabinet, I'll be back tomorrow to fix it up,' Slim said.

'You're a gentleman. Not had one of those in my life since poor Den passed.'

'I've got plenty of time on my hands.'

Clora laughed. 'I guess it must be hard to find people to interview in a little village like this.'

Slim shrugged. 'Most people don't want to talk to me. And those who do don't have much to say.'

'About Den?'

'About anything.'

'Perhaps you're not asking the right questions.'

Slim was quiet, sipping his tea. 'I'm not sure what questions I should be asking.'

'Well, you think he's alive, but everyone round here thinks he's dead. If he was alive, where's he been all this time, and if he wandered off somewhere for a while, why'd he come back? Why now?'

Why now. Slim leaned back on the armchair, resting his head against a headrest that smelled of damp. Why now indeed.

'I've got to make a phone call,' he said, standing up.

'Well, you'd better hike up the hill a bit, as you'll get nothing down here.'

Slim nodded. 'I'll be back in a while.'

Clora just shrugged and reached for the TV remote. 'Any time. I'm not going anywhere, am I?'

'I'VE GOT NOTHING SUBSTANTIAL FOR YOU YET ON that abattoir,' Don said. 'A negligence case from 1988 where an employee fell off a ladder while at work. Case dismissed. The employee in question wasn't wearing the required safety shoes. The company was covered by warning signs in the workplace and a line in the employment contract.'

'A name?'

'Adam Black. Retired in 1994. Died two years later of a heart attack while on holiday in Germany. And before you ask, I checked it out. Nothing suspicious. He'd had heart trouble for a while and keeled over one evening after a long day of hiking.'

Slim nodded. 'Keep trying. In the meantime, I've got a couple more for you, dates this time. The first is September 6th. It was the date Ozgood was supposed to deliver the money, according to the first blackmail message. I need to know if that date has any significance. It could be a clue. Den's death, the fire that killed his brother, a significant date in the abattoir's history. Something like that. The second was October 2nd. He didn't pay up then, either. Anything at all '

'Okay, on it. I'll add the fee to your tab, as always.'

'Thanks.'

Don hung up. Slim looked around. He had been walking while he talked and had come to the outskirts of Scuttleworth. A farm lane led off to Slim's right. A public footpath access sign poked out of the grass nearby, so Slim went that way, preferring the open space of fields to Clora's cluttered flat, the cold looks of the village residents, and the claustrophobia of the woods.

The lane wound uphill between two hedgerows, turning a corner and opening out onto a muddy farmyard. A couple of chained dogs barked at him. A handful of cows behind a gate gave a tired series of moos. A man walking across the yard gave him a brief wave then disappeared into a barn, rolling up sleeves of a check shirt as he went, Wellington boots squelching in the mud.

Another footpath sign pointed between two outhouses, directing Slim to a stile crossing into a field. A well-trod path led along a hedgerow in an upwards direction, angling for the hill's crest and a small fenced-off area containing two picnic tables.

Slim climbed over. A herd of cattle far across the field gave him bored stares as they chewed sods of grass. The ground was boggy by the foot of the hedgerow so Slim took a more circuitous route out across the grass. Above the hedge, the view opened out. The village lay below him to his left. Then, as he reached the tiny viewpoint, the landscape to his right appeared, the other valley turning Scuttleworth's hill into a diamond, with Ozgood Hall on the neighbouring hilltop to the east. From here too, to the south, the passing duel carriageway was visible, and the overpass bridge where, in less than two weeks, Ollie Ozgood was expected to leave two million pounds in cash inside a leather bag.

Slim frowned, wondering if Dennis Sharp had stood right here as he made his plan to coerce his former employer.

He wiped moss off one of the picnic tables and pulled a notebook out of his bag. On the latest page he had written:

Reasons for Dennis to blackmail Ozgood:
His own supposed murder.
His interference into the relationship with Ellie.
Something to do with the fire and his brother's death.
Something else?

Slim frowned. His analysis seemed woefully inadequate, and not for the first time in his career as a private investigator, he felt the pang of imposter syndrome. He shouldn't be here. He should be lying in a gutter somewhere, booze-soaked, drinking away the crumbling remains of his existence.

There was something, though. A missing link, an unexplored path.

Ellie Ozgood.

35

THE COMMUNITY HALL WAS EMPTY. SLIM WENT INTO the kitchen, smiling at the coffee brand Mandy had bought to replace the one Slim had finished off. One he had suggested. He wondered if she had ordered any surplus for Cathy to sell in the shop.

He set the kettle boiling and went into the little library to continue perusing the old parish council notes. He found more files like the one he had looked at, dating back more than thirty years, to when crusty sheets of paper—adorned with Tippex—had been typed up on a typewriter.

Slim wasn't sure what he was looking for as he slowly read back through the notes. He remembered what Kay had said about finding a sample of text for syntax comparison, but Slim didn't get the impression that Dennis Sharp had been much of one for writing articles for the parish council magazine.

After a fruitless hour, he remembered the boiled

kettle and took a coffee out to the terrace. His hands were beginning to shake with withdrawal pangs, but the weather had taken a cold turn so he pulled up his sleeves and let the wind chill the internal discomfort of his body. As always, it took a few minutes of hard willpower just to remain in the chair and not run like a maniac for Cathy's shop or the village pub, but after a while he began to settle. He stared out at the valley, wishing a helicopter would appear, dragging a signboard announcing the location of Dennis Sharp's hideout.

He felt better after the coffee so went back inside. A sudden thought struck him, so he searched through the files until he found dates around the fire that claimed Steve and Colin. It had been too much to hope for some hidden clue, but he did find a couple of notices about the funerals for each boy as well as a later memorial service for both, then a fundraising coffee morning to raise a donation towards their headstones. There was no speculative message about the cause of deaths, but the minutes a couple of months later carried a note about the town council's plan to pull down the ruins—there was mention of a memorial playground which must have never happened—and then a month after that an official letter from Michael Ozgood apologising for the situation and promising a full safety inspection of all Ozgood-owned buildings in the Scuttleworth area.

Slim rubbed his eyes. He felt the beginnings of a headache that was another sign of his enforced withdrawal, plus a rumbling of his bowels which suggested his body's cravings wouldn't give him up without a fight. He turned a page to read just one more month's minutes, and paused, staring in surprise at the mention of a familiar name.

Article 14: a letter was received this morning from Dennis Sharp, officially resigning from his voluntary position of games keeper. It was suggested by Councillor Winston that requests for the position be considered, but in the absence of a volunteer, the position be officially closed. Councillors in agreement: 9. Councillors against: 0.

Slim put the file down and looked up. Would Sharp's resignation letter be on file somewhere?

And what was a games keeper?

It only took him a few minutes of back-reading to figure it out. Prior to the fire, each parish council magazine contained a short advert for a games night right here in the community hall, two Tuesdays every month. All kinds of family board and card games would be available, including chess, Monopoly, Scrabble, Risk, battleships, and more. The evening's host: Dennis Sharp.

It made sense that Dennis's resignation had come after the police investigation's conclusion and his clearance from suspicion. From subsequent magazines and council notes, it was clear no one had come in to fill Dennis's position.

Slim whistled through his teeth. Fifteen years ago. Dennis Sharp had been twenty-nine years old, a local boy, employee of Ollie Ozgood, and involved with village life. The fire and the suspicion fallen on him had pushed him to the fringes of the community, a man who lived and worked in the forest, out of sight, out of mind. How had Dennis reacted to his sudden ostracising? Had he suffered it, embraced it, or had it turned him bitter, resentful? Had he blamed Michael Ozgood or the Ozgood family as a whole? Had he targeted Ellie, Ollie's teenage daughter and the Ozgood heiress, as a way of exacting revenge? Or had he been thinking bigger, holding out perhaps to marry her, tie himself to the Ozgood empire which had caused his social downfall?

Slim's head was spinning with more questions than he could comprehend. The answers, though, felt one step closer.

36

'MY CONTACT SAID WE HAVE A MATCH.'

Croad's grin was as wide as it was sinister. 'Now all you have to do is catch the bastard to save my boss a lot of money and make a lot for yourself.'

'My contact would prefer the original documents, though. Also, if you could find something that Dennis might have written—a letter or a work report, even—it would help a lot. His analysis isn't foolproof, and it certainly wouldn't stand up in a law court.'

Croad glowered. 'I don't think Mr. Ozgood is interested in it going that far.'

Slim held back the rest of his suspicions. If he mentioned seeing Sharp in the forest it might inspire Croad to demand long, rambling walks in the woods together.

'And I still want to talk to Ellie. Dennis might have contacted her.'

Croad glared at him. 'Mr. Ozgood said to stay away

from her,' he snapped overly loudly, then mouthed, 'I'll ask.'

Quoting jobs to attend to, Croad left Slim alone, his crabby old car misfiring as it took on the hill out of the valley. Slim sat at the table, massaging his temples, considering his next move.

Croad remained an enigma too. Was the old man on Slim's side or not? All the evidence pointed to both. Croad seemed to support Slim's investigation as long as it didn't encroach too much on his master's territory, which by very definition made him a hindrance. Getting some time with Ellie Ozgood was key, but from his behaviour it seemed more than Croad's job—or possibly even his life—was worth. If Slim was going to speak with her, he had to manufacture a situation independent of Croad's involvement.

He headed back to the village, puffing as he crested the brow of the hill. He wanted to speak again with Mandy, if he could find her. Cathy was a decent second option, with her knowledge of the parish council, so he turned up the main street towards the shop, but as he rounded a corner, he heard a vehicle coming up behind. He ducked into the hedge, only for the builders' van to pull in ahead of him.

The driver's door opened and Jimmy Kent climbed out. Sober, Slim felt no threat from the scrawny, angry young man. However, as Jimmy approached, the back doors opened and two others emerged, both of a similar age. One wore jeans and a black t-shirt, the other a skintight white vest under an armless body warmer. Crewcut, tattooed and frowning, they looked like building site bruisers. Slim tensed, wondering if they'd dare jump him in the middle of the street, and if they did, which one he should go for first to give him the best chance of getting away.

'Been looking for you,' Jimmy said, stopping a couple of steps out of punching range and stabbing a melodramatic finger at Slim's chest. 'Went past your place but you weren't home.'

Jimmy's henchmen moved wider, flanking him, ready to spring if Slim bolted. Slim kept his gaze on Jimmy, but balanced his weight so if could move to meet whoever rushed him first.

'We got off on the wrong foot,' Slim said, wondering if Jimmy's anger could be defused with a simple apology. Jimmy, though, gave a sudden frown as though processing the information was impossible.

'I don't know what you're doing round here, but I think you ought to pack your bags and get going,' Jimmy said. 'Asking questions about stuff long over is only going to upset people. Who do you think you are, asking my dad about my brother? You upset him bringing all that up, and I don't like seeing my dad like that.'

Certain Kenny Kent could speak for himself, Slim said, 'I'm sorry about that, but it was a simple enquiry connected to an investigation. Once I'm done, I'll be gone and you'll never see me again.'

Jimmy tensed like a spring ready to bounce. 'I think you're done now.'

Slim smelled no alcohol on any of them. He knew Jimmy was the key. Diffusing Jimmy would keep the others off him, but if Jimmy boiled over, the others would likely pile in, and he'd have a brawl to contend with.

'I'm not done now, but I will be soon. Perhaps you could help me yourself. You're a local guy. You must know something.'

'I'm not saying anything to you!'

'I don't want to know much. Nothing about Colin.' He risked a glance at the others. 'Have you ever sat in the hot seat?'

Jimmy frowned. He glanced at the others, but the one on the left had flinched, one closed fist involuntarily rubbing his stomach as though he'd felt a sudden itch.

'What's he talking about, Kev?'

The one called Kev grimaced. 'He means Sharp's old motor. Down there in the woods.'

'That?' Jimmy snorted. 'Load of rubbish.'

'So you haven't?'

'Course not.'

Jimmy was defiant, but Kev looked ready to bail.

'What happened?' Slim asked, addressing him directly.

'Heard voices—' Kev started, but he was cut off as Jimmy barrelled forward, shoving Slim in the chest, tripping him up. Slim hit the ground and rolled, getting out of kicking range, sitting up in time to see Jimmy advance a couple of steps, fists clenched, face scrunched. The other two hung back behind him, the third man unsettled by Kev's submission.

'I don't want to see you round here anymore,' Jimmy shouted. 'Next time I'll do you proper.'

He waved a fist, a phantom punch. Then, with one

last scowl, he retreated to the van, the others following. Kev gave Slim a sympathetic look just before he climbed in.

Slim climbed to his feet as the vehicle roared off, brushing himself down. He let out a long breath, his heart thundering, his hands shaking. He had escaped unharmed, but it appeared Jimmy Kent was a person to avoid.

A shame, Slim thought, as he headed for Cathy's shop, as he felt it likely Jimmy would have a lot to say.

37

'YOU'RE BECOMING MY MOST REGULAR CUSTOMER,' Cathy said, as Slim put a tin of ravioli down on the counter. 'I'm wondering if I should give you a locals' discount.'

'Is there such a thing?'

Cathy laughed. 'No. But I might invent one. It depends how long you stick around for. You know, I actually did a stock check the other day. Haven't you heard about home delivery? The rest of the village is crazy for it. Either that or they hate me. Honestly, every time I see one of those Morrison's vans I'm inclined to throw a rock at it.'

'I suppose they're just lazy. Nothing to do with you.'

'Thanks.'

'I heard you used to be on the parish council.'

Cathy frowned. 'Where did you hear that? God, not for years. Not since my boy was born, and since I realised it was an exercise in wasting time.'

'Why's that?'

Cathy shrugged as she shook her head. 'This village isn't what it used to be. We have nothing for tourists like the coastal areas do, so it's always been quiet. But you know, it was all right when I was growing up. There's barely half the people around now, though, and those that are left seem resentful that they're still here. Plus, when something happens like when those two boys died, it sours everything for years afterwards.'

'You mean Steve Sharp and Colin Kent?'

Cathy gave a sad smile. 'So, you've found out about all that?'

Slim nodded. 'A tragic accident. Must have been terrible for the mothers. I heard Shelly Sharp never recovered.'

'Shelly Holland,' Cathy said, correcting Slim's deliberate mistake. 'She went into a spiral after that, for sure. I sometimes think Mary was lucky in a way, doing what she did.'

'Mary?'

'Mary Kent. Oh god, you didn't know, did you? She took her own life a couple of months after Colin died. She couldn't handle the grief. She left Kenny to bring up Jimmy on his own.'

Slim wanted to bury his head in his hands, wishing he could take back ever visiting Kenny Kent. 'That's terrible. I didn't know.'

Cathy gave him a sideways glance as though to suggest he was lying, then added, 'She was well-liked around here. A lovely lady. Very pretty, always outgoing.'

With a grin, Cathy added, 'Way too good for Kenny Kent.'

'He seemed nice enough to me.'

Cathy rolled her eyes. 'We called him all sorts behind his back at school because he was so boring,' she said. 'He was forty before he was twenty, if you know what I mean, but Mary seemed to like him.'

'I guess you never know how things will turn out,' Slim said.

'You're not married, I take it?'

Slim sighed. 'Divorced. She ran off with a butcher. I got thrown out of the army for trying to kill the wrong man.'

'Oh. I guess that didn't turn out too well,' Cathy said, grinning as though Slim were telling a joke. 'No children, I take it?'

Slim remembered a long-ago letter he had pulled from a rubbish bin while staking out his ex-wife. A notification of a successful abortion and the passing of a test that showed there would be no complications in later pregnancies.

'No,' he said quietly, thinking of what might have been. 'Unfortunately not.'

Nathan suddenly bustled through the door, dressed in a navy blue school uniform. He sighed dramatically at his mother, snatched a chocolate bar off the rack and moved on through into the house like a passing tornado.

'Ah, you're not missing much,' Cathy said.

Slim had once dreamed of having a beautiful little girl to bounce on his knee. 'I doubt it,' he said, unable to meet her eyes. Then, wanting to change the subject, he lifted the can of ravioli and said, 'I don't suppose you could heat this up?'

'Ten pence extra,' Cathy said.

'Really?'

'But five for you.' She winked. 'Locals' discount.'

38

It had started to rain while Slim was in the shop. The community hall was uncharacteristically locked, and the pub—despite Slim's reluctance to enter its hallowed doors—didn't open until six, so he found himself sitting inside the church porch with a plastic tub —which he had promised to return to Cathy later—of warm ravioli on his lap as the rain came down and a gradual darkness descended.

The church's porch had a single seat made of a slate slab, freezing cold to the touch. After a few minutes of bearing the chill to the back of his thighs, he shifted, attempting to fold the lapels of his jacket up underneath him. As he moved, he felt something shift in his pocket, and he pulled it out to examine it.

The doll Shelly had thrown that had cut his face, the same one he thought that she had thrown at him on the day of their first meeting. He turned it over in his hands. Made from sticks bound together with wire, the face bore little carved eyes and a nose, but the mouth was covered by a strip of cloth tied at the back. Dust engrained into the nicks in the wood told Slim it was old, but even though it had frayed and faded over the years, Slim could still guess that the light blue colour had indicated a doctor's mask. Indeed, on the now-naked body there were wisps of thread which suggested the doll had once been fully clothed.

Slim frowned. Why then, if it had supposed to have been a doctor, did its hands appear to be tied?

He had at first thought one of the arms had broken, but now he saw that the break showed some signs of cutting. Both arms had been bent behind the doll's back and tied with wire.

A doctor with his arms tied, or a prisoner, gagged and bound?

Or both?

Slim put the doll back in his pocket. Alone, it had no meaning, but if it had been part of a tableau of other dolls, Slim might be able to figure it out.

Shelly had thrown it at him. Did she have more?

The rain had stopped. Slim finished his lunch and ventured outside. In the overflow graveyard, Shelly's tent glistened with fresh rain. Slim stopped far enough away that he could easily retreat if Shelly sent forth another projectile. He took out the doll and held it up.

'Shelly,' he called quietly. 'Shelly, are you in there? I'm back. It's Slim. Talk to me, please. I think Dennis is still alive. I saw him in the woods.'

At first nothing happened. Then, as though a calm day had decided to turn to storm, a rising shriek came from inside the tent. At first it sounded like a distant siren. Then it rose in pitch until it was unmistakable: the cry of a woman overcome with grief.

Slim took a step forward, then laid the doll down on the path and turned to walk away. He had nearly reached the gap in the hedge when the rustle of plastic made him turn. Shelly stood there, outside the tent flap, an elderly woman dressed in rags, her greying hair disheveled, small eyes darting around as though she'd just woken from a long sleep and was seeing the world for the first time.

'Be leaving if I were you,' she said, her voice a gravelly rustle that sent shivers down Slim's back. 'Poison in this village, poison in everything. Poison by the name of Ozgood.'

Then she was gone, back into the tent, the door flap billowing briefly in the wind then falling closed behind her.

39

Kenny Kent was just switching off the lights when Slim knocked on the door.

'I came to apologise,' Slim said. 'I was out of order the other day.'

Kent frowned, as though apologies weren't something he often heard. He pulled the door shut and locked it before turning to face Slim, who had retreated down the steps and out of punching range.

'You went off the rails, there, didn't you? Not seen the lad riled like that. I got him calmed down but he wouldn't tell what had happened between you.'

'It was nothing,' Slim said.

'He's a bit wild at times, but it looked like you have a gob on you too.'

'I was out of order. I'm sorry. I hoped we could finish our conversation.'

Kenny jangled his keys and slipped them into his

pocket. 'We're closed. I wouldn't say no to a pint, though.'

'I'm an alcoholic.'

Kent began to laugh. Slim assumed the builder had thought him joking, but then Kent said, 'That explains it. You didn't like the sweetener I added, did you?'

'It got in the way of my recovery a little.'

Kent slapped Slim on the shoulder. 'Well, I'm sorry about that. I tend to self-medicate myself—have done for years. I keep my head when I need to use it, and the lad drives us everywhere. Losing my wife and kid so close together … screwed me up a little. I imagine you've heard by now that my wife died not long after Col?'

Slim considered feigning ignorance, but wasn't sure he could pull it off. 'People in backwaters like this like to talk,' he said.

'Figures,' Kent said. 'Not a lot else to do round here.' He sighed. 'Let's just say that those few months after that fire were a bad, bad time.' He looked up, his eyes suddenly sparkling. 'But, what doesn't break you and all that, right? And I had to stay strong for the boy. He's not perfect, but I did my best. Did what I could on my own.'

While speaking, Kent had led Slim around the back of the work yard to a plain bungalow set at the back of the grounds. He unlocked a front door and led Slim down a hall into a kitchen, switching on lights as he went. Slim noticed the signs of a masculine life unintruded on by women: copies of *The Sun* lying open on the sofa, piles of unwashed plates in the sink, a sock hung over the back of a chair. It felt familiar; his own life had been much the same before he found himself homeless, with the minor exception that he didn't read newspapers.

'Excuse the mess,' Kent said with a nonchalant flap of his hand and a tone that suggested he said it twenty times a day. 'Find somewhere to sit down. I'll make you a brew.' Then with a grin, he added, 'I'll leave yours plain, although I'm not expecting Jimmy this evening so you're probably safe. He lives over in Harton, raising hell over there, no doubt.'

'I bumped into him earlier,' Slim said. 'He politely requested that I leave the area.'

Kent rolled his eyes. 'I'll have a word with him. He's out of order saying things like that.'

'He's technically right. I'm an outsider. I'm on Ollie Ozgood's payroll. That makes me the enemy, doesn't it?'

'A lot of us have been on that prick's payroll at one point or other. It's all very well having standards, but when someone has money and you don't … so what is going on? I know you're sworn to secrecy, I imagine, but….'

'Someone claiming to be Dennis Sharp is blackmailing Ozgood, demanding large sums of cash to keep quiet about something I know nothing about.' Slim took a deep breath. 'Dennis is supposed to be dead. I've been given proof. But, there's evidence to suggest otherwise. I … I even think I saw him.'

Kent had taken a seat across from Slim. He paused, frowning deeply. 'I probably shouldn't have asked.'

'You don't think it's possible? Not at all?'

Kent didn't smile. 'No. No, I don't.'

'Because when the dead are dead, they stay dead? Because—'

Kent closed his eyes, lifting a hand at the same time to cut Slim off. 'No, because if by some miracle Sharp wasn't dead, Scuttleworth is the last place he would come.'

'His family is here.'

'What family? His brother is dead. His estranged mother is a raging lunatic. His father is long gone.'

'What about Ellie?'

'Ellie Ozgood?' Kent gave a bitter laugh. 'She might have been a worthy conquest, but a reason to come back?' Kent shook his head. 'Perhaps you should go and meet her then come back and tell me whether she was a woman worth returning from the dead for.'

'What's wrong with her?'

'Money tends to ruin people. Ellie Ozgood is a perfect example. The girl has never done a day's hard work in her life, yet she has everything she could ever want. You think she's qualified to run Vincent's? She's twenty-two. She does nothing in there except sit in an office and boss people around.'

'Doesn't that describe most managers?'

Kent laughed. 'Yeah, but usually they have to earn the right to be an arsehole with a few years company service. You know what they said about her, don't you?'

'What?'

'That Ozgood only put her in there to stop her spending his money. Girl did her typical private school education then got shipped off to university where she blew a wad of money doing god knows what. Ozgood paid her way through a couple of years of failure but they threw her out in the end. He holed her up in Vincent's as a way of trying to reform her.'

Slim gave a slow nod. 'So if Dennis came back, you don't think he'd contact her?'

Kent shook his head. 'I think he'd run a mile in the opposite direction.'

40

Evan Ford didn't look pleased to see Slim as he entered but he still stood up and shook Slim's hand before waving him to a seat.

'I wouldn't normally be allowed to do this but Ollie Ozgood asked me personally,' Ford said, sliding a folder across the table. 'These are Dennis Sharp's autopsy and notes on the investigation.'

Slim opened the file and slid out a number of printed photographs as well as a couple of stapled documents. The first few pictures showed Dennis Sharp's crashed car from multiple angles. A couple of things immediately struck Slim as odd.

The first was snow on the ground surrounding the car. The second was the burned dash and scorched paintwork.

Slim pointed both out to Ford. 'The crash happened in late December,' Ford said. 'It was raining on the day but we had had some early snow a few days before.

There had still been patches of ice under the trees and on the road down into the valley where Dennis was killed. Before you ask, yes, it was considered as the cause of the crash. However, far more likely is simply that Dennis was driving too fast. The car broke through a great deal of foliage on its way down into the woods, although the impact was what killed Dennis, when the car struck the rock.'

'No airbag?'

'The car was an old model.'

'Head injuries?'

'Extensive. Dennis wasn't wearing a seatbelt and went through the windscreen. The fire from the engine igniting only caused problems with identification.'

Slim frowned. 'No one told me he was burned.'

'Excuse me, but why should they? You're not police.'

Evan Ford's tone was condescending, but Slim let it pass. Playing the bumbling supposed city lawyer might work to his advantage.

'If he was burned, surely that would put a question mark over his identification?'

Ford rolled his eyes. 'You watch too much television. Yes, he suffered some burns, but he wasn't exactly chargrilled, for heaven's sake,' he said with a flippancy that made Slim wince. 'And it was his mother who identified him.'

'His mother, who's half mad?'

'She was a lot less that way before the death of her firstborn,' Ford said, in the same school teacher's tone that made Slim want to slap him. 'His clothing was consistent, as were certain body markings. Birthmarks, moles, that kind of thing.'

'But no DNA?'

'It isn't required when a body is positively identified by next-of-kin,' Ford said. 'I know you'd love for his death to have been faked, but this isn't a television show.'

'I don't think his death was faked,' Slim said, even though his mind had begun to whirl with fanciful ideas. He had learned from previous cases never to discount any possibility.

'I won't ask you what you do think,' Ford said. 'It wouldn't matter anyway. The case is closed, a simple one of driving without due care or attention.'

'A couple more questions, if you don't mind,' Slim said as Ford shifted in his seat and glanced towards the door. 'And the car … it was checked?'

'It was inspected for faults. An old car like that likely had a few, and that's what was shown—soft brakes, a corroded transmission, two tires that would have failed an MOT, had Sharp done one—which, by the way, he hadn't; his car had an-out-of-date certificate. All in all, there were lots of problems with that car, but nothing that didn't agree with general wear and tear. It was a death trap waiting to happen, frankly.'

'Anything else? Anything suspicious or unusual? What was in the car?'

Ford leaned forward. 'Now, there's an interesting question. You know, Mr. Hardy, for a bloodsucking lawyer it seems there's a bit of detective in you after all.'

Slim was tiring of Ford's tone. His head had begun

to pound with another withdrawal headache, and his bowels were tightening up. He gave Ford his best smile then said, 'I suppose just a bunch of gardening tools.'

Ford laughed. 'Of course. A lawnmower, a set of pruning shears … and two skinned lamb carcasses.'

41

I<small>T HAD STARTED TO RAIN AGAIN, SO</small> E<small>VAN</small> F<small>ORD</small> reluctantly gave Slim a lift back to Scuttleworth. During the brief journey he told Slim how the police had spared Sharp's family and friends any embarrassment by quietly having the carcasses disposed of with Ollie Ozgood's agreement. To have Sharp—who had already been a polarising figure—posthumously charged with sheep rustling would have brought unnecessary shame on his grieving mother.

'Ozgood at first wanted the man charged,' Ford said. 'He relented when we pointed out that his death had probably been punishment enough.'

He dropped Slim at the corner by the church and drove off with an unnecessary 'Well, I hope this is the last I see of you.' Slim stuffed his hands into his jacket pockets as the car headed up the street, to resist giving Ford a shaking middle finger. In truth, he would also be happy not to cross the old policeman's path again, but he had even more questions now than when he'd set out for the meeting.

Had Sharp been involved in the theft and resale of sheep carcasses from Vincent's? It seemed ridiculous, but unless meat theft was a common practice in Scuttleworth, Slim needed to identify and contact the man he had seen hiding in the forest as soon as possible. It seemed likely he had known Dennis Sharp, or even been in league with him.

Slim took shelter in the church doorway again, pulled out his phone and called Donald Lane.

'Any luck?'

'Nothing yet. I'm still trawling. Things going okay down there, Slim?'

'I'm getting there. The usual way, getting into trouble angering people.'

'Just be careful.'

'I will. Can you do something else for me? I'd like you to investigate Oliver Ozgood directly. In particular, I'd like to know when he was in and out of the country over the last few years.'

Don laughed. 'Would you like me to spy on your mother-in-law while I'm at it?' Then, after a pause, 'I'm just joking, Slim.'

Slim smiled. 'Far as I recall she's been in the same place for the last twenty-five years,' he said. 'Although I wouldn't put it past her to come back from the dead. I owe you, Don. I owe you again.'

'Ah well, I'm not exactly run off my feet these days. Take care, Slim. I'll be in touch.'

The rain had eased, so Slim walked up the street to a

phone box outside the pub. Inside, it still had a ragged phone book tied to a shelf by a piece of string, so Slim rifled through it until he found the name he had memorised from the top of the car mechanics report.

Joe Taber. A local mechanic from Harton who had inspected Dennis Sharp's car. From the sanctuary of the phone box Slim tried to call on his mobile, but Joe didn't answer. Slim saved the number to his phone's contacts list and headed back outside. To his relief the rain had eased, reverting to a fine mist which left visibility down to a few metres.

Theories were beginning to swirl, and formerly safe places had begun to feel threatening, so Slim headed for Clora's, where, as he had hoped, she welcomed him in on the condition he make the tea.

'People are going to start to whisper about us,' she said, the conspiracy in her words negated somewhat by her eyes not looking away from a TV quiz she had consented to turn to a lower volume. 'Well, they would, if anyone around here was watching.'

As Slim passed Clora a mug and then sat down with his own, he said, 'That's something I wanted to ask you about. This might sound stupid, but how do you feel about the Ozgood's?'

'Useless wastes of space,' she snapped.

Slim frowned. 'Deeper than that. How do they make you feel? Are you afraid of them?'

Clora actually turned away from the TV to look at him. She cocked her head, wrinkling her nose. 'That's a strange question. There's only the two of them left, Oliver and Ellie.'

'As best as I can figure it out, they own more than half the total commercial land in the Scuttleworth area. Not so much the people themselves, but the Ozgood name. Its associations. How does it make you feel?'

Clora bit her lip. 'Honestly?'

'Honestly.'

Clora wrinkled her brow, considering. She squinted up at the ceiling, then turned to look at him.

'Uncomfortable,' she said.

42

SLIM MUSED ON CLORA'S WORDS AS HE WALKED BACK in the twilight to his cottage. She had tried to elaborate on her feelings without much success, but Slim had got the impression he expected. It was helping him build up a clearer picture of the Ozgood family's influence on the local area, and tallied with the impressions he had picked up elsewhere.

The family was a looming presence, one that imposed influence in ways few could clearly define, like having a stain on the back of your shirt—there, even if you couldn't see it, preying constantly on your mind. People acted accordingly, and over the years they had bent under the patriarchal pressure without even being aware of it.

On the way back, just before his phone signal cut out, he called Croad.

'I need a list of employees at Vincent's,' he said.

'Everything you can get me. Names, addresses, ID photos if you have them.'

Croad's response was a low growl, followed by a single word. 'Impossible.'

'No, it's not. You're Ozgood's right hand man. You've delivered so far. I think the blackmailer might be on the staff.'

'What makes you think that?'

'I'd rather not say until I'm sure,' Slim said, stalling for time, fearing Croad would call his bluff. 'I need a couple of days to figure things out.'

'I'll ask Ellie.'

'No, don't ask Ellie. Ellie is the last person I want you to ask.'

'Why?'

'I haven't talked to her yet. I'd rather keep her out of everything if I can. Isn't that what Ozgood wanted?'

Croad reluctantly agreed. He hung up, grumbling about doing what he could.

It was getting dark. With the forest closing in, Slim wanted nothing more than to lock all the doors, pull a duvet over his head, and forget about everything, but he sensed that as much happened in Scuttleworth at night as it did during the day, so he pulled his jacket on, ready to head back out.

He couldn't do it alone, though, so he took one of the 35cl bottles of brandy he had bought from Cathy's shop and slipped it into his pocket. He had chosen the smallest bottles on sale because he knew that once he broke the seal he would drink everything, but he could still function if he kept his intake to a sociable level, and it would give him just enough courage to do what needed to be done.

He had cracked the bottle within a few steps as the forest and all its menace closed in, and drunk everything by the time he crested the hill out of the valley to find a three-quarters moon above him, its pale light a comfort after the oppressiveness of the forest.

Somehow he had taken a wrong turn, and instead of emerging in Scuttleworth as he had planned, he was standing on a quiet lane surrounded by farmland, with Ozgood Hall visible through the hedgerow to his left.

As the crow flew, it was barely half a mile, so Slim walked until he found a gateway then climbed over into a field.

With the moon lighting his way, he stumbled along the hedge to the field's end, then clambered up a muddy slope in the corner and dropped down into the adjacent field. His head was spinning as he crossed the last field bordering the manor house's grounds.

It rose ahead of him, three floors of ornate balconies, tall windows and white-washed walls. Slim felt like Gretel as he scrambled through the last hedge, eager to see up close a place outwardly beautiful which might prove to contain nightmares he could barely imagine.

As he tumbled out of a stand of hawthorn onto a manicured lawn, his first thought was how a burglar might feel standing here. There seemed to be no guard dogs, and Slim guessed Croad acted as security. The cameras attached to each corner blinked with lights likely designed to advertise their presence and dissuade any opportunists.

All of the lights barring a couple on the ground floor were off, and one higher on the second. Curtains closed off the lower windows, too thick even for shadows, but the light was stronger from the upper, suggesting the curtains were open.

Three oak trees rose not far from the hedgerow. Slim stared at them, estimating the height of the upper branches. About level. High enough to see inside.

It was a stupid idea and he knew it, but the sober, reasoning part of him was locked tightly away for the night. Slim grinned as he approached, gauging the difficulty of getting up into the lower branches from the branchless lower trunk.

His luck was in. A shed stood nearby, its door open. A coil of electric cable hung on a nail just inside, caught in the only patch of moonlight.

He used the cable to create a brace to get up into the lower branches. From there, climbing was easy, even as his vision spun from the exertion. Reminding himself repeatedly that he was taking a terrible risk yet at the same time not caring, he hauled himself up through the branches until he was level with the second floor window.

A bedroom. A tangle of sheets topped a double bed, pushed out slightly from the wall as though someone had thought to move it and then changed their mind. A red carpet, grey curtains pulled open, a teak desk against one wall, a wardrobe against another, half open, an untidy disgorgement of clothes spilling from inside like the lolling tongue of a strangled beast.

At first Slim thought the room was empty, then the

tangle of bedclothes shifted and a naked woman appeared. Slim didn't know where to look, but she bent and picked a night dress off the floor, slipping it over her shoulders. Even before she approached the window Slim knew this was Ellie. She was the same height as the girl he had seen, was the right age, had Ozgood's hair colour and a set about her face that suggested power and calm.

She opened a pair of balcony doors and stepped outside. She wrapped her arms around herself but stood there in her nightdress for some minutes, staring out into the dark, her gaze cutting right through where Slim crouched among the tree branches, not daring to move.

What was she doing? What was she looking at? Slim was desperate to shout out to her, to ask, only the barest scraps of sobriety keeping his mouth shut. Even so, he was on the verge of just doing it anyway when the bedsheets moved behind her.

'Shut that damn window,' came a familiar voice. 'It's getting cold in here.'

Slim hardly dared to breathe. As Ellie stepped back to close the doors, her expression unchanging, a naked figure rose out of the bedsheets, and in the instant before Ellie jerked the curtains shut, Slim caught a glimpse of Thomas Croad.

43

ONE THING SLIM HAD COME TO LIKE ABOUT Scuttleworth and its surrounds was that people enjoyed their coffee. Whether it was a need to stay awake in an otherwise dull patch of middle Devon or something else, he appreciated it as Joe Taber poured him a thick brew and handed it across the table. Slim, nursing a hangover, but also proud of himself for not immediately reaching for a bottle upon waking after what he had seen last night, clutched at it like a drowning man for a piece of driftwood.

'A private investigator, you say?'

'Yes. I work for the BBC,' Slim added, preparing to unravel the spiel he had used on previous cases to get quiet men to talk. 'There's been some interest in a documentary on the Ozgood family, and our researchers came across the twin tragedies of the Sharp brothers, Steve and Dennis.'

'Well, I couldn't tell you much about Steve. Didn't

even live down here then. Moved down in 2007. The yard was going cheap, fancied a quieter life.'

Joe Taber was a thickset man in his late fifties. He wore greasy overalls with the comfort of a man who could have been born in them. Wide spectacles were constantly pushed up a shallow nose above a mouth that had a permanent downward droop, making Taber look miserable unless he openly smiled.

'You were called to examine Dennis Sharp's car, weren't you?'

'That's right. Closest guy around and I'd seen plenty of wrecks up in London. Held some authority in a backwater like this.'

'I'd like to know how that went, if there's no problem with you talking about it.'

Taber shrugged. 'Didn't you get a look at the police report?'

'Yeah, I did. I just wanted to hear it in real time.'

Joe gave half a shrug. 'Not a lot to tell. They called me up, had me drive down there, look over it, see if the crash was caused by anything mechanical. The fuel tank had burst, the igniting petrol setting fire to the dashboard and the seats, but there was nothing particular wrong with that car besides its age. It was a junk heap. I heard Dennis Sharp rarely drove, so it was likely he wasn't familiar with the ice on the road. A lot was made of his supposed local knowledge, but as I said, he wasn't much of a driver. Plus, he'd gone through that barrier at speed, judging by the impact damage to the front bumper and radiator. Reckless speed, if you ask me.'

Slim leaned forward. 'Is there any possibility that the car had been tampered with?'

Joe Taber frowned as he shook his head. 'I don't know what kind of TV shows you watch, but the kind of tampering you're suggesting just wouldn't work in a practical sense. Sure, if you know what you're doing, you could strip down the wires to the brakes, make them liable to fail, but you'd have no way of knowing when they might fail. They could go slowing into a junction, and what point would that have?' He sipped his coffee. 'In any case, I did take a look. Nothing had been done. It was just bad luck, poor maintenance, and reckless driving.'

'According to the police report, Sharp was doing approximately forty-five when he hit that barrier.'

Joe Taber clicked his fingers. 'Exactly. You go and take a spin along that road. Let your brakes off after that last curve at the top there and see what natural speed you get. Nope, he was accelerating into that corner as he hit the ice. Makes any tampering to the brakes irrelevant.'

'So you think it was completely innocent?' Slim said.

'Oh, I never said that,' Joe said, 'and I would have told them if they asked but none of the police down there cared for my opinion.'

'And what was it?'

'That he hit that barrier and crashed because he had someone on his tail. He was being chased.'

44

'I DON'T SUPPOSE MANDY'S ABOUT?' SLIM ASKED Cathy as he paid for a can of all-day breakfast and a packet of Worcester Sauce flavour crisps. 'I just wanted to ask her something.'

'Don't have designs on my daughter, do you?' Cathy said, lifting an eyebrow.

'Pretty sure she wouldn't be interested in an old pensioner like me.'

'Well, there's no one around here of her own age I'd approve of,' Cathy said.

Slim smiled. 'That Jimmy Kent seems like a nice boy.'

Cathy rolled her eyes. 'Kid's a brainless thug, just like his dad.'

'It must have been hard for Kenny after what happened to his wife and child,' Slim said. 'Bringing up a son as a single father can't have been easy.'

Cathy shrugged. 'I guess I'm a little hard on him. It's

funny, but old stereotypes from school never go away. He's all right, is Kenny. I'd have a friendly word if he ever came in my shop.'

'Perhaps you should consider, um, restocking from time to time?'

Cathy cocked her head. 'Look at you, the big city guy telling us village idiots how to run our businesses.' She smiled. 'You have to balance it right, otherwise the wrong people start to show up. I'm happy to pass the time with old Helen from down the road but the last thing I want is to have to make small talk with Oliver Ozgood, or even worse, that ghastly Thomas Croad.'

'That bad, is it?'

Cathy sighed. 'It's bad enough my husband working at Vincent's.'

'Isn't there other work in the area?'

'Nothing without a decent commute. Although, there are times when I wouldn't miss a few extra free hours each day.' Before Slim could reply, she added, 'The truth is, we've talked about it, and while I'd like him to go elsewhere, he says he's happy enough. It's not easy work, as you can imagine, but he's satisfied with it, and the pay's not bad.'

Slim nodded. 'I guess that's something.' He handed her a five pound note. 'If Mandy comes back in the next half hour, tell her I'll be over at the community hall.'

'You planning on moving in?'

'If I can find a barn with the right sized hayloft, I'm thinking about it.'

With his all-day breakfast slowly cooling in a plastic tub, Slim headed out. He was only halfway to the community hall when his phone rang. Putting his lunch down on the edge of a stone wall, he plucked his phone out of his pocket.

He frowned, hesitating to answer. Croad. What if the old man knew what he had seen?

He was still thinking when the call hung up. A second later his phone began to ring again, so this time he answered.

'Yes?'

'Where've you been? I got a call from Mr. Ozgood. He wants an update. It's only a week until November 9th, the date in the letter. You made any progress?'

'Some. Doing what I can.'

'I'll be over there at three. I need something concrete to show Mr. Ozgood. His patience won't last forever and I think he's starting to panic that there'll be no progress. Your head's on the chopping block.'

Slim suppressed a sigh. 'All right.'

'Good. See you there.'

Croad hung up. Slim scowled at the phone, wishing the old man would stay out of his way. He had done little to help and now it seemed there was a conflict of interests. Was he protecting Ellie for Mr. Ozgood or for himself?

Slim gave a slow nod. It was time to take things up a level. He called up an old friend. 'Alan, it's Slim. How are you doing?'

Alan Coaker, a former platoon mate of Slim's, had formed a locksmith's merchant in London after leaving the army. Unlike a regular locksmith's, it also branched out into rather more high-tech security equipment.

'Slim, good to hear from you. It's been a while, and I always wonder if you're still alive.' Alan gave a gravelly cough. 'What are you after?'

'I need a favour.'

Alan laughed. 'There's a surprise. Let me guess, you want me to extend you some credit like last time?'

Slim grimaced. 'I'd much appreciate it. I'm good for it, I promise. I'm working for a rich man this time around.'

Alan sighed. 'I like you, Slim, which is why I always hope you're right. Okay, tell me what you need.'

After Slim reeled off his requests, Alan sighed. 'You don't ask for much, do you? Just this once. Consider it a rental, so I want it all back undamaged. Got it?'

'Sure.'

'I'll order a courier. It'll be down there this evening. Let me know where it ought to be sent.'

'Thanks, Alan. I owe you one.'

'One?' Alan laughed. 'I think we're in double digits by now.'

45

THERE HAD TO BE A CLUE SOMEWHERE, SLIM thought as he leaned over his notebook. He had filled three pages so far with lists of names and events as he slogged his way back through old parish council magazines. It might be nothing, but there could be a clue hidden in among the notes to someone's involvement in something. Cathy, for example, had led monthly litter-picking events for nearly five years, before abruptly quitting. Her replacement, a lady named Tina Tremlett, had lasted only three months before handing it over to someone called John Dovetail. A clue, a hint at something, or just part of the ever present shallows of the river of country life?

After three coffees and two hours of note-taking, his eyes were starting to blur, so he put the magazines aside and flicked through a couple of picture books he had found.

The light was already fading. One more day almost

gone, less than a week until the supposed deadline. What would happen if Ozgood failed to produce the money? Would Dennis Sharp appear out of the shadows like a contemporary Robin Hood to shoot down the landowner with an arrow between his eyes?

There was little Slim felt sure of, besides one or two minor things that likely had no bearing at all.

He was looking through a book of old local primary school pictures when he heard the main doors open with a creak. Mandy appeared, hands in the pockets of her jacket, the bulge around the zip hiding a more incendiary bulge beneath.

'Heard you was looking for me.'

Slim looked up. 'I just had a couple of questions.'

'Like what? I might have been busy.'

Slim smiled. 'Sorry. I imagine life is pretty hectic around here.' As Mandy rolled her eyes, he added, 'First of all, do you know Jimmy's friend Kevin?'

'Kev? Yeah. Why?'

'Do you have a contact for him? I'd like a word with him about something he said.'

'Got his Facebook.'

'I'm old fashioned. Do you have a telephone number?'

'What do you think I am, the Yellow Pages? Look, give me your number and I'll pass it on.'

'Thanks.'

As Slim fumbled for his phone, Mandy sauntered over, peering over Slim's shoulder.

'What you looking at pics of primary kids for? You some kind of perv?'

'No, I'm—'

'Whatever.' Mandy started laughing. 'That's me, see there. Pretty, weren't I?'

Slim looked down at the grainy class photograph, estimating the blonde girl with the beaming smile to be nine or ten. He then looked up at the current version. She had soured a little, but the prettiness was still there.

'You haven't changed all that much.'

'Just doubled,' Mandy said, patting her stomach.

'There is that,' Slim said. He lifted the book, a collection of local school class photos dating back several decades. 'Some of them are dated, but most of them don't have names,' Slim said. 'Do you think you could find Dennis Sharp?'

'I could have a look,' Mandy said. She sat down, opening the book in front of her. 'I remember these pictures were donated by locals,' she said. 'There was this guy compiling local information for a history book, something like that. Don't think he ever finished it.'

'Why not?'

Mandy shrugged. 'Think he died. I'll ask Mum. She'll know. Ah look, here we go. 1986. I think he was a bit younger than me mum, so he'd have been in school in this pic.' She slipped a slightly faded picture out of its plastic jacket, turning it over. 'You're lucky. This one's labeled. That's him there, third from the left.'

She turned the picture over, handing it back to Slim. The boy was about eleven, blond, tall for his age, but already broad shouldered. The other kids all had their arms straight, but Dennis had his hands clasped together as though unsure what to do with them, and while the boys on either side wore broad smiles, Dennis just stared straight ahead.

'Mum said he was a real heartbreaker. You can see it, can't you?'

Slim frowned. 'He looks familiar.' He flicked forward a few pages to the pictures he had been looking at when Mandy arrived, ones that were clearer and had better colour. 'There,' he said, pointing at a boy standing on the end of a back row. 'I'm guessing that's his brother, Steve. Sorry, half-brother.'

Mandy stared at the picture for a long time before she looked up. Her face wore an expression somewhere between defeat and regret.

She gave a slow shake of her head, followed by a sigh.

'No, that's not Steve. That's Colin Kent.'

46

MANDY DIDN'T WANT TO TALK ABOUT IT, MAKING HER excuses and leaving. By the time Slim packed up and made it to the shop, it had shut early, a cardboard sign in the window apologising for a family emergency, maybe due to design, maybe not. Slim didn't dare talk to Kenny Kent, and he didn't even want to see Croad, even though they had an arranged meeting. He considered going to see Shelly again, but the churchyard seemed imposing and he'd had enough of getting hit.

Clora welcomed him with her usual request for a cup of tea. A crumb-covered plate suggested some bread product had been lunch, and Slim dutifully washed it in the sink before returning with two steaming mugs.

'Colin Kent was Dennis's son,' he said by way of greeting as he settled into an armchair.

Clora sighed. 'So I've heard whispered over the

years. I never asked him and he never told, but I knew Mary used to religiously take Colin to games night at the community hall. Whether that was a cover for letting Colin meet his real dad, I don't know.'

'Does Kenny know?'

'Who knows what he suspected and what he knew? Colin's been dead fifteen years. Don't dredge this up, Slim. You'll only hurt people. All three of those involved have gone, and Kenny's a decent guy. He doesn't need this brought up again. And it has nothing to do with this blackmailing business, does it?'

Slim wondered otherwise, although there was no clear connection.

'To be honest, I'm no closer to figuring anything out.'

Clora rolled her eyes. 'You think you're being all detective, but tell me something you've found out that isn't just an unearthed village rumour that's been allowed to lie.'

'I now think Dennis Sharp is dead.'

Clora laughed. 'I thought you thought he was alive?'

'I've changed my mind.'

'Well, there's genius at work right there. How much is Ozgood paying you? I think I might apply for a job.'

Slim finished up his tea and left. The mockery in Clora's tone had got to him, even though deep down it was deserved.

He headed back up to Scuttleworth and called Don.

'I need something else,' he said, as Don came on the line. 'This could be important, or it could be a waste of time.'

'Thanks, so you're passing it on to me?'

'Um, yeah. I'll get you back for all this, I promise.'

'Go on, shoot.'

'I need the coroner's report on Steve Sharp and Colin Kent.'

'Wow, easy. Anything else? The queen's birth certificate?'

Slim ignored the sarcasm. 'A list of Oliver Ozgood's employees for which income tax was paid. Ideally going back twenty years or so. Also, while you're at it, anything else there's a significant tax record on Ozgood for. Large purchases, donations, things like that.'

Don was quiet a moment. Then, 'All right. I'll do what I can.'

Slim stepped back as he hung up, getting onto the verge as a slick Ford four-wheel drive vehicle came around the corner. At the wheel, Kenny Kent gave Slim a wave, slowed as though to stop, before seemingly thinking better of it and speeding away.

It was nearly half past two. Something about his frustration with Croad made Slim feel like running the old man late. He headed back to the community hall, made a coffee, and retrieved the book of school photos.

Colin Kent appeared in four. Always standing, he appeared to shoot up as the years passed, losing his puppy fat, and indeed his smile, on the way. By the final photograph, taken just weeks before his death, he was a scrawny, dour kid. In contrast, Steve Sharp, labeled a few spaces along in one picture where he wore a beaming smile, looked lively, full of life.

Slim stared at the photograph, willing it to reveal its

secrets. Finally he shook his head, closed the book and put it back on the shelf.

A blackmailer. *Don't forget,* he reminded himself. He was supposed to be hunting a blackmailer.

CROAD HAD A FACE LIKE THUNDER. 'SO, WHAT YOU'RE telling me, is that six days before all hell is set to break loose, you still have no idea if Dennis Sharp is alive or dead? Have you learned nothing? Nothing at all?'

Slim found it hard to speak to Croad. He wanted to reveal what he had seen, expose the old man, uncover what betrayals, unions, or sacrifices were being made by a young heiress bedding her father's old caretaker.

'I have several ideas, but I need more time.'

'You don't have any. Do you think this is just a game?'

'I'm doing my best. Did you get me that list?'

Croad grunted then pulled a crumpled sheet of paper out of his pocket and threw it down on the table. 'That do? I couldn't get pictures, but that's all the names.'

Slim picked it up. Around twenty-five people. Mostly names he'd never heard of, but there were some he had—

Cathy's husband Tom, and a few others from the parish council notes. Tina Tremlett was noted as "production line assistant", and John Dovetail as "deliveries manager".

'Thanks,' he said. 'It's something to work with.'

Croad grinned. 'He one of those? The blackmailer?'

Slim saw an opportunity to set a lie that would at least keep Croad off his back while he figured things out. 'That's what I think. I think it's someone close to Ellie. Someone who might know what she knew about Dennis Sharp.'

He watched Croad's expression, but if the old man suspected he had fallen under the radar of Slim's suspicion, there was no sign. Slim could almost believe Croad's liaison with Ellie was entirely innocent.

'Anything else you need?'

Slim nodded. 'Yeah. A lift.'

'What?'

'I'm expecting a delivery at the post office in Harton. It'll be shut by the time I walk there.'

Croad looked pained but nodded anyway. 'Let's go, then.'

The old Marina cranked into life as Croad worked the gears. Slim patted the ancient car on the door, feeling the hinges slip under his press.

'How old is this thing?' he asked as the car suddenly misfired with a loud crack. 'A hundred years?'

'Had her fifteen,' Croad said with a sense of pride, stamping the accelerator as the car threatened to stall during the hill climb. 'Done me proud.'

'Doesn't Ozgood pay you enough to get it fixed?'

'It's character,' Croad said. 'I remember this time back in the reserves—'

'Hey, isn't that the way down to where Dennis died?' Slim interrupted, pointing at a turning that sloped up and over the crest of a hill. 'Mind if we have another swing past?'

'If you're sure your post office won't shut,' Croad said.

'We're good for a while,' Slim said. 'If you could step on it a bit that might be useful, though.'

Croad scowled. He put the old car into first then swore as he made the turn, the front bumper scraping the hedge. 'Used to be cut back a bit more,' he said as he accelerated up the slope before slowing again as the car reached the first bend angling down into the forest.

'Isn't that your job?'

Croad grinned. 'I'm overworked.'

The forest appeared around them. Croad, scowling as though feeling every bump on his skin, carefully negotiated the steep curve into the forest then pointed as the corner where Dennis Sharp had crashed came into view up ahead.

'Clever of Ozgood to know the exact point when Dennis's brakes needed to fail,' Slim said, as Croad paused briefly before making the turn and heading on down the hill toward the ford. 'I mean, with the roads around here, they could have failed at any time.'

Croad pulled the car up just short of the ford. Slim waited for him to reverse into the turning space on the river's right side, but instead he turned to Slim.

'I've told you to watch your mouth,' he said. 'Someone could be listening.'

Slim rolled his eyes. 'Who's going to have bugged your car?'

'You never know. Just keep your mouth shut about all that.'

'You know what I think?'

'What?'

Slim hesitated. Letting Croad know one of his theories was a huge risk, but it could work in his favour.

'I don't think there was any tampering done to the car. I think Ozgood ran him off the road, then let his little theory get around to build up his aura a little bit. It works in his favour to maintain a little fear among the community, doesn't it?'

Croad shook his head. 'You're crazy. Ozgood was wasting his time hiring you. If it was up to me, I'd kick you back to the street where you came from and hire someone with a decent track record.'

'A good job it's not.' Slim tapped the dashboard clock. 'Is that thing on time?'

'Ten minutes slow, give or take.'

Slim swore. 'Post office shuts at five. I need that delivery today.'

Scowling again, Croad turned the car around and headed back up the hill. He slowed briefly at the crash corner, frowning as he stared into the trees, perhaps wondering if Slim's theory had any weight.

They reached the post office with just a couple of minutes to spare, Slim feeling increasing frustration at Croad's excessive caution down the country lanes. Alan, despite a shaky track record of sometimes playing tricks on Slim in the past, had seemingly come through this time: three heavy boxes waited for Slim's collection.

'What's this?' Croad asked, turning one over.

'I can't tell you right now but I'll be charging any breakages to Ozgood.'

Croad gave him a lift back. He pulled up outside the cottage and looked ready to leave, but Slim asked him to hold on while he unloaded the parcels. After safely locking them inside the house, he climbed back into the car.

'What are you doing?' Croad said. 'I thought we were done.'

Slim shook his head. 'It's nearly half five,' he said. 'Perfect timing to meet Ellie after work.'

48

WITH THE EXCEPTION OF HIS VERY FIRST MEETING with Ollie Ozgood, in the three weeks he had lived in the forest outside Scuttleworth, this was Slim's first time inside Ozgood Hall. As he sat in a reception room, his inappropriate attire for such an elegant place negated somewhat by Croad's even scruffier appearance, he could only marvel at the untold wealth layering itself around him. Like a living museum, Ozgood Hall was wealth on top of wealth, tall ceilings and opulently sculpted walls surrounding antique furniture, musty wall hangings, and intricate, faded paintings.

On his way in, Slim had passed through a more service-like entrance and glimpsed kitchens and a lounge more modern in style, but a sense of being out of place infiltrated every pore of his being.

Then there was the feeling of anticipation. Ellie Ozgood was the forbidden fruit, the-one-that-must-not-be-involved. Slim had images of dragons, demons, and apparitions coming through the door, so that the girl herself, when she finally appeared, could never possibly live up to his expectations.

He heard the taxi stop outside. The door opened. Croad's muffled voice. Footsteps, then more doors opening. He stood up. Ellie marched into the room. She threw a bag over a chair before she even looked at him. Croad was hovering at her arm, looking so awkward that Slim couldn't possibly imagine them as bed partners. Surely he had been mistaken. Then Ellie turned to him, and the coldness in her eyes sucked the heat out of the room.

'John, isn't it?'

'Most people call me Slim.'

Ellie nodded. 'So, you're my father's latest game.' She turned to Croad and asked for tea. Slim stared in disbelief as she actually snapped her fingers, as though calling a dog to attention.

'Mr. Hardy prefers coffee,' Croad said.

Ellie just shrugged. 'Bring whatever.' She took a chair opposite then waited for Croad to disappear before speaking. Slim struggled to associate the waif-like girl he had seen by the window with this hard-faced version who seemed old beyond her years.

'It's a wonder it took you so long to come and see me, since I'm at the centre of it all,' she said.

'I was warned off. I think your father wanted to protect you.'

Ellie sighed. 'The story of my life. My mother passed away when I was very young,' she said. 'And with no other siblings, he was always obsessively protective.'

'You said he was playing a game? What does that mean?'

'All this about some blackmailer.' Slim must have looked surprised, because she added, 'Oh, did you think I didn't know? Of course I know. I'm practically my father's secretary. Do you know how many of these things he gets? There have been half a dozen this year already.'

'So why did he think this one was different?'

'Because, like most people, he's scared of ghosts.' She shrugged. 'Do you even know where he is right now, while his whole empire is supposedly under threat? South of France. Some villa even I've never been to, most likely with some woman barely older than me. Does he seem concerned? You tell me you're not part of some stupid game.'

Slim leaned forward. 'I can only do what I was asked to do,' he said. 'Do you think it's possible that Dennis Sharp is still alive?'

Ellie's countenance darkened. 'There's no chance. That's just a story. If Dennis was alive I'd know it.'

'And why's that?'

Ellie looked about to reply when the doors opened and Croad came in, carrying a tray of drinks. Slim noticed he had changed his shirt and even appeared to have brushed what was left of his hair.

'Thank you,' Ellie said dismissively, not even glancing up at Croad. He lingered a moment, then realised he wasn't welcome and withdrew. Ellie pulled her seat closer to Slim's and whispered, 'I guess he was told to keep you away from me.'

'Something like that. He seems protective.'

'He's my father's hands. He'll do anything my father asks.'

Slim took a sip of his coffee. It was sweet and weak, the opposite of how he liked it.

'I was hired because your father thinks Dennis Sharp is still alive. The letters held information no one else could know.'

Ellie laughed, a cold, bitter sound. 'Anyone could get a copy of the police report. It wouldn't be hard. I imagine you've seen it, haven't you?' When Slim didn't answer, she continued, 'I don't know what he told you, but it wasn't rape. I liked Dennis. I seduced him.' She glared at Slim. 'Isn't that what bored, wealthy daughters do?'

'If that's what you say. I haven't met any others.'

'My father found out. He fired Dennis, but where was Dennis supposed to go? He grew up here, in the oppressive shadow of Ozgood Hall. My father made him homeless, kicked him out. My father wanted him convicted, but it wasn't going to happen. I was only just sixteen. At first I felt coerced, but as time dragged on, I realised I could walk away and nothing would befall me.' She shrugged. 'So I did.'

'But Dennis died.'

As though Slim had found a chink in her armour, Ellie looked down, staring at the floor.

'Yes, he did,' she said at last.

The question burned on Slim's tongue, leaving him no choice but to ask it. 'Do you think your father was involved in Dennis's death?'

Ellie was silent a long time. Slim was beginning to wonder if she'd even heard the question when she looked up and said, 'No, I don't. But he wishes that he was, and there are people around here who think that he was, and he's happy for them to think that.'

'Nothing like holding a healthy dose of respect for the local lord,' Slim said.

'Said like a true pauper,' Ellie answered, even adding the hint of a smile. 'If you want my advice, I'd pack my bags. You'll find nothing but unhappiness here.'

Ellie seemed finished with the conversation. She made some excuse about work to do then called for Croad. The caretaker dutifully appeared, gave Ellie a respectful nod then led Slim out to the waiting car. Its engine was running, the inside still warm as though Croad had anticipated he would soon be needed. A chilly wind had begun to whip through the trees, and as they entered it, the forest filled Slim with dread.

Croad dropped Slim off outside his door, muttered, 'I told you it was a waste of time talking to her.' He then added something about coming by tomorrow. Slim nodded and got out, waiting as the car drove off.

He knew before he entered the house that someone had been inside. He had stuck a piece of loose tape to the bottom of the door handle, and it had fallen to the floor. Inside, the hall looked the same, but the documents he had left on the table had been moved slightly. He had left two sheets of paper, one angled to the other but with an exact one centimetre distance between the two corners. Whoever had been inside had attempted to hide their passing, but not quite been accurate enough, the ruler Slim pulled from his pocket showing an extra half centimetre.

He had talked to Ellie for about thirty minutes. Croad would have had plenty of time to drive back down and have a look through Slim's things. The car had been running when he went outside, but Slim had not heard it from inside the house.

Croad was too obvious an answer, though. He had time to come down here and get back, but how could he have known how long Slim would spend talking to Ellie?

But if it wasn't Croad, who could it have been?

Behind him, the front door creaked, suddenly inching open. A gust of wind blew through, disturbing the papers on the table. Slim was sure he had closed the door, but it was loose on its fittings. Perhaps no one had been inside the house after all. Perhaps the wind had shifted the papers and was playing tricks with his mind.

He moved to shut it, but as he did it shifted a little further.

Something lay on the mat outside.

A tingle of fear ran down Slim's back.

A tiny doll, made out of twigs and straw.

49

WITH THE ONE-OFF EXCEPTION OF THE OAK OUTSIDE Ozgood Hall, Slim hadn't done much tree-climbing since his army days. Luckily those surrounding the cottage had a lot of low branches, and once he was off the ground he found things easier. Still, by the time he had rigged the two motion-sensor cameras and suitably concealed the power cables he attached by an illegal socket to the power line accessing the cottage, his arms and back were aching.

One viewed the front, the other the back. Triggered only by motion, they accessed via a cable Slim fed through a bedroom window a program on a computer tablet Alan had also provided. The screen was dark, but when Slim went outside and waved his arms about, he came back in to find a few seconds of recorded footage.

He hid the tablet under his bed then ate lunch out of the box of provisions Ozgood had ordered for him. Unanswered questions continued to stack up, but Slim felt close to a breakthrough. If it was Dennis Sharp out in the woods, the cameras would show if he tried to get into the cottage. And if it was Croad after all, he would know that also.

He read over the list of names Croad had provided. It didn't surprise him not to find Ellie among them; he had long surmised that her position at Vincent's was an unofficial one. In order to hunt the man he had seen with the sheep carcass, he needed to add faces. He could get no WiFi signal in the cottage so he put his old laptop in a bag and headed up to the community hall.

He was just reaching the brow of the hill when his phone rang. Two rings, then it hung off. The number was unrecognised, so Slim called back.

'Yeah? What do you want?'

Kev. Borderline hostile but lacking the same conviction as when he had been with Jimmy.

'It's Slim Hardy. Do you remember me? You nearly kicked my arse.'

'Um, yeah, well—'

'Look, I don't care about what happened. I just want to know more about something you said.'

'I didn't say nothing. Jimmy did all the talking.'

'Yeah, you did. When I asked about Dennis Sharp's old car in the woods, you said—'

The phone line went dead. Slim stared at his phone, suspecting the battery, but his old Nokia still had a couple of bars. Kev had just hung up.

Slim called back. Kev answered on the fourth ring.

'Sorry, I just—'

'Tell me what happened.'

'I don't want … I mean—'

'Just tell me. I'm not going to go snitch to Jimmy, or tell any of your mates. I just want to know what you were going to say about that old car.'

Kev sighed. 'Look, I was drunk. It was one of those kid things. We all went down there, chugged some Diamond White, whatever. The boys dared me to go sit in there.'

'The car?'

'Yeah. The front seat. Driver's side.'

'And you did?'

'Yeah, course. I ain't no wimp. The boys waited by the road. It was afternoon, like, wasn't proper dark. I could see the boys cheering me on so I wasn't scared.'

'And so you got in the car?'

'Look, if you tell anyone about this—'

'I won't.'

'I don't want no one saying I was a wuss because I weren't.'

'I know you weren't.'

There was a long pause. Slim looked at his phone, but the call was still live. He wondered if Kev had put the phone down and walked away.

'Kev?'

'Yeah, I'm here.' A long sigh. 'I … I sat in that seat and someone spoke.'

'What did they say?'

Kev groaned as though his confession were physically painful. 'I was drunk, like, so I could have just imagined it. But it sounded like, "Get out of here".'

'And what did you do?'

'What do you think I did? I ran like a bastard.'

'You didn't see anyone?'

'No. Only the boys when I got back to the road.'

'What happened?'

'They thought I was full of crap. A couple went down but nothing happened. Reckoned I made it up, took me years to live it down. Wasn't the only one though so I know I wasn't crazy.'

'Not the only one?'

'Yeah. Loads of people have sat there and heard it, just no one'll say. Don't want to look like they're mental.'

After making Slim promise again to keep quiet, Kev hung up. Slim carried on to the community hall. Inside, he set up his laptop and went through Croad's list of names, searching for each across various social media sites. Most had an online profile somewhere, but none of those he found matched the face of the man he had seen in the woods. He had narrowed it down to about half by the time he decided to take a break.

He took a coffee out onto the back terrace and sat gazing down into the forest. What further secrets did it hide? Was Dennis Sharp down there right now, hiding out, or was he really dead after all? Slim could no longer be sure either way.

He pulled the second doll out of his pocket and turned it over. It was crude, the kind of thing a child might make in art class: limbs stumpy, an over-large head, a press of cotton wool on its neck where an attempt at hair had failed.

Slim frowned. If Dennis had left it for him, it had to be for a reason. It was either a hint at something, or a warning. If Dennis was playing a game, it had no logic. The figure had to have something to say.

The door to the terrace opened suddenly, surprising him. Mandy leaned out, holding a duster in her hand.

'Thought it was you.'

'Just getting some air.'

Mandy's gaze moved to the table and Slim realised he'd left the doll in view.

'Where'd you get that?' she asked.

'Uh, I found it.'

'Out the back?'

Slim stared. 'There's more?'

'Boxes of them. Old stuff from one of those fetes. They keep anything nice that doesn't sell if they have room. I had to go through it all once, give it a clean.'

'Could you show me?'

'Sure.'

Mandy led Slim through into a storeroom behind the library. The cramped, windowless space was piled high with community junk: fold-up tables and chairs, boxes of Christmas decorations, wooden skittles pins, even what looked like a small bouncy castle stuffed in a corner. With Mandy offering instructions, Slim dug his way into the back and retrieved two sunken cardboard boxes.

'Pretty sure they were in there,' Mandy said.

Slim took the boxes through into the main hall and put them down on a table. The contents were a mixture of homemade jewelry and little wooden figurines, the detail on most far better than the one Slim had found, as though the creator had let his skills go to seed.

'Who made these?' Slim asked, certain he already knew the answer.

'Most were done by Dennis Sharp, but a few of these were other local kids. He used to do the odd workshop, if I remember right,' Mandy said, picking a cow made of twigs out of the box and holding it up to the light as though to examine it. 'I mean, I don't remember much but there was a craft table at the parish Christmas festival and Dennis was sat there, showing kids how to make them. I had a go. Got my picture taken for the magazine.'

Mandy was beaming, staring off into space. Slim looked up. 'Any chance you could hunt out a copy of that magazine? I'd love to see it.'

Mandy nodded, but her smile had faded. 'I remember there was some trouble. A bit of a commotion. I don't know what about.'

'With Dennis?'

Mandy nodded. 'Someone started shouting at him, so he got up and left.'

'Do you remember who?'

Mandy shook her head, tossing her hair back. 'How would I know? I was still in primary school.'

'And you're seventeen now?'

Mandy pouted. 'Nearly eighteen.'

Slim looked at the teenager with the strands of pink hair and the pregnancy bump and felt a sudden pang of regret. His own child would have been of a similar age by now. Would he have had a daughter? Someone with a skewed view of the world who needed his protection?

And if he had, what would she think of him, a

stumbling, homeless drunk slowly blagging his way through each day?

'Stop looking at me,' Mandy said. 'Are you drunk again?'

Slim felt the press of an unopened bottle in his pocket. 'I quit,' he said. 'I think.'

Mandy grinned. She reached into her pocket and held out an empty cigarette packet. 'I quit too. I threw the last ones away. I keep this to remind me.'

'Good for you.'

Mandy patted her stomach. 'I told you. I'm gonna be a good mummy.'

'And what about the father? Have you told him yet?'

Mandy scowled. 'I don't want to talk about it.'

'He deserves to know.'

Mandy shrugged. 'Maybe.'

Slim decided not to press her. 'Let's have a look for that magazine.'

They found it in a book of a years' worth bound together. The parish Christmas festival was a four-page colour pullout. Most of the pictures were of various stalls and displays, but there were a couple of the mingling crowd.

'That's me,' Mandy said.

She was kneeling on a blanket laid on the floor in front of a table covered with little wooden dolls. A string of tinsel hung along the table's bottom edge. On the blanket were various items used in the construction of the dolls: twigs, nuts, pieces of wool, and a couple of glue guns to stick it all together. Another older boy was sitting beside Mandy, while behind them a man was leaning over, half obscuring the display.

'That's Jimmy,' Mandy said with a petulant hint to her voice as she pointed to the boy. 'Our first meeting, I suppose.'

'And that's Dennis Sharp?'

'Yeah.'

At the back of the display, a handwritten sign read, *Woodwork of the Forest*, while beneath it was taped a smaller piece of paper with more description, too small to read.

'Is that sign still back there?' Slim asked, feeling a sudden flush of excitement.

Mandy shrugged. 'Might be. I'll go look.'

As she wandered off to the storeroom, Slim picked a couple of the dolls out of the box and put them down on the floor, matching them to the ones in the picture.

One was lying down, its arms over its head. Another was leaning forward, looking at the first one's stomach. In the background, something on all fours lay beside a clump of white cotton.

Slim frowned. It was a tableau of some kind, perhaps a scene from a book or a local story.

'Got it,' Mandy said. 'This what you were after?' She held up a browned square of paper. 'It was crushed at the bottom of the box.'

'That's it, thanks.'

Slim practically snatched it out of her hands, turning it over to read. Some of the words had faded and a corner had broken off. It was a simple paragraph talking about man's connection to the forest. Slim spotted a couple of spelling and grammar errors but it was the note itself that had him excited.

Kay Skelton was a trained forensic linguist, his field of specialisation after leaving the army. But even Slim, an amateur at best, could see the handwriting on the note was completely different to that on the message received by Oliver Ozgood.

50

SLIM SAID GOODBYE TO MANDY AND HEADED OUT. HE tried to call Kay but his friend didn't answer, so he left a message. Back at the cottage, he found the copies he still had of the letter and the work ledger and compared them with the paper from the woodwork display, doing his own analysis. There was a clear difference.

But if Dennis hadn't filled in the ledger, who had?

There was an obvious answer.

The man who had slowly taken over Dennis's job.

Croad.

Slim felt an immediate sense of discomfort. He went around the house, checking the locks on the windows, peering into every cubbyhole as though expecting a bogeyman in an old soccer shirt to come jumping out. Remembering the cameras he had set up, he retrieved Alan's tablet from under the bed and accessed the saved information, but aside from a crow which had used the doorstep as a nutcracker for a few minutes, only his own return had triggered the sensors.

Nothing.

He had left his phone on a window ledge, and as he sat down at the table it buzzed, startling him. With just one signal bar flickering on and off, it had been unable to maintain enough signal to receive a call, but it had nevertheless caught a voicemail. Slim picked it up. Not Kay, Don.

He tried to call back, but today he was unable to get enough signal, even when he stood on a chair and held the phone up to the ceiling. He wanted to know what Don had to say but couldn't face another uphill hike into Scuttleworth.

He pulled out the folder of maps Croad had left and looked one over. He could reach a field edge if he headed straight through the forest behind the house and then headed uphill.

And if he continued on in a leftward arc, he would reach the road that led up to Ozgood Hall, entirely bypassing a hill in the middle.

He frowned.

'Huh.'

Still frowning, Slim found a ruler and laid it across the map, nodding as the measures confirmed what he had suspected. It made so much sense now. Dennis Sharp's cottage was down a meandering road to Scuttleworth's south, leaving him an awkward drive or a long up and down walk to work. Dennis, however, not being a man of civilisation, would surely never have taken a narrow, winding road if he could go quicker through the forest. Cutting through the trees, following a river north and then hiking up through forest to the back of Ozgood's estate, the route was less than half the journey as that by road.

Slim packed a bag, keeping the bottle in his pocket for safekeeping, and headed out. He soon found himself in a section of the forest he had not been in before. The trees closed in through a steep-sided gorge, rocky outcrops outlining a dry riverbed which connected to the stream. Near the water Slim found signs of regular passage. Near a couple of larger pools in which trout glided lazily, he found items of fishing tackle left behind as though for explanation, trod into the mud.

It was all too mundane, too serene. Slim slowed his pace, squatting low every few steps, pausing, listening, looking for something out of place, something that shouldn't be.

He had just intersected with Dennis's likely route up to Ozgood Hall when he spotted it.

In a patch of mud, pointing away from the river, uphill into the thick, seemingly impenetrable thicket of brambles and low-lying hawthorn, a single boot print.

His heart screamed at him to follow the direction of the print up into the thicket, but the old soldier in him retained more sense. Keeping low to the ground, he looked around, assessing from which angles he was covered, from which he was exposed. If someone had a gun trained on him right now, where would they be holed up? If there was surveillance equipment, where might it be?

Back across the river, the undergrowth was thinner,

the fallen leaves crisp enough to betray an observer should they make any movement. Slim slowed his breathing, cutting out all unnecessary sound, tuning himself to the forest. Up and down the stream the path angled out of sight, leaving few viewing places, while an observer from the thicket above would have to watch through several metres of tangled vegetation.

Careful not to move any other part of his body, Slim twisted his head and looked up into the branches overhead.

Nothing.

Satisfied he was unobserved, he considered the possibilities.

A single footprint ought to be harmless, perhaps left by a walker peering uphill, assessing the possibility of a way through. But from the depth of the sole mark compared to the heel, Slim could tell the person had pushed off, climbing up the slope.

Slim looked around for the best option to follow, spotting a gully of exposed rocks that shifted around the edge of the thickest brambles. Moving slowly and as quietly as he could, he followed the rocks, staying off the leaves where possible. The rocks rose up out of the gully until he reached a point where he had to jump back down. He now had a rocky wall on one side, a tangle of brambles on the other. A thin gap lay between, so Slim squeezed through, emerging in an open plateau with a carved rocky slope on one side and a mass of brambles on the other.

The bowl of rocks rising around him had an artificial look to it. Slim sensed he was in an ancient quarry, perhaps one begun speculatively and later abandoned. As he followed the rock wall he saw bore holes from a drill in some of the breaks in the rock.

And against a slope steep enough to act as a back wall, he found a small, abandoned brick building.

Three walls remained, the other covered with a black plastic sheet. The roof had been replaced by a couple of pieces of corrugated plastic. No attempt had been made to hide that someone was squatting here: a square of broken bricks was filled with fire ashes.

Slim lowered himself to the ground, felt around under the leaves, and pulled out a fist-sized rock. Holding it like a club, he approached the hut's front.

No movement came from inside, and as he skirted around the opening, he saw the hut was empty.

Someone was definitely squatting here, though. A green sleeping bag lay in one corner, while a table made with bricks held a plastic bag of wild mushrooms.

Slim lifted the bag, turning it over. The man he had seen, it had to be.

A crunch came from behind him. Slim spun, catching a glimpse of a shadow bolting between the trees.

'Dennis, wait!'

Too late, the man was gone. By the time Slim had reached the break in the gully, all that was left of Dennis Sharp was the faint, receding crackle of running feet on leaves.

Slim threw his bag down, swearing as he did. Dennis would no doubt go to ground, perhaps find somewhere else to hide. Slim had missed his opportunity, but on the off-chance Dennis returned, he pulled a piece of paper from his bag and scribbled a quick note.

I mean you no harm. He paused, then added: *I'm on your side.*

He put it on the bag of mushrooms and headed back to the river. As before, Dennis had left no trail to follow. Slim looked along the river, but Dennis, it seemed, had already staked out where the dry ground that would leave no tracks lay.

Slim threw the rock he was still carrying to the ground, kicking at the leaves in frustration. His original purpose forgotten, he headed back to his cottage. The bottle was in his hand without him realising it was there, half of the liquid inside him with no remembrance of it going down. The cottage appeared out of the forest like a shimmering mirage, and if Slim hadn't been walking with his head lowered, he might have missed the figurine lying on the mat entirely.

He scooped it up and examined it, wishing his vision would stop wavering. It was smaller than the previous one, its body scorched as though by fire, its twig arms aloft.

'You're trying to tell me something, aren't you?' Slim whispered, aware as he entered the little dining room that the papers were no longer properly aligned, but already too drunk to know if any had been taken.

He slumped down on the bed, feeling like a failure. Dennis Sharp seemed to be looming above him, multi-faced, some expressions laughing, others scowling, others with eyes filled with tears.

51

ANOTHER MISSED CALL HAD SNEAKED THROUGH. SLIM, teasing down a coffee to medicate a beastly hangover, sat at the table in the living room, trying to make sense of everything.

He had three dolls now, two men, and a burned boy. They were all crudely made, as though Dennis's skills had gone to seed in the six years since his death.

The cameras had been triggered. Slim had copied the feed file on the tablet and transferred it via a USB to his old laptop, which now sat open in front of him. A bird had at some point alighted on the one trained on the entrance, knocking it slightly askew, so that the view of the approach was half what Slim had wanted. The first couple of triggerings had been by birds, followed by one from a wandering cat, so Slim skipped to the end, where the figure of a hooded man could be seen taking the last few steps to the door and then bending down, standing up again, leaning close to the door, and then going inside. A minute or so passed before the figure re-emerged, did something to the door—presumably locking it—then disappeared from shot.

Dennis Sharp, it had to be, leaving clues and then checking on Slim's progress.

Slim needed a drink. He had drunk his small supply dry but could find more booze in the village. Getting out of the trees would also clear the encompassing foreboding that now felt all around.

He took the road. Cathy said nothing as he bought a bottle of brandy and a tin of beans and sausages. When Slim asked her to heat it, she said, 'If you drink that first you won't need it heated,' which Slim took as a refusal and stumbled out of the shop, his fingers already working the bottle cap. He drank half the brandy on the way to the small village green, where he tried to sit on a bench but slipped off, ending in the grass alongside.

His phone jabbed into his hip, and he remembered Don had tried to call him. He had another missed call too, this one from Kay. Afraid of what Don might say, he called Kay first.

'Yeah? Slim, you all right? You don't sound good.'

'I fell off a bench.'

'Is that all?'

'Playing it by ear. One step at a time.'

'Forwards or back?'

Slim wanted to answer sideways, but was gripped by a sudden fit of laughter.

'Slim? Are you okay? Perhaps a bit of time off the case might help. Why don't you come down to London for a bit? I could put you up—'

'Three days,' Slim said. 'My deadline.'

'Why did you call?'

Slim remembered. 'I found something. A sample of Dennis Sharp's writing from an old parish Christmas festival. It doesn't match the ledger or the note. It's not him. He's not the blackmailer.'

'Are you sure? Can you send me a copy, or if possible the original?'

'Sure, I....' Slim trailed off, remembering the table, the adjusted papers, seeing now what was out of place, what was missing.

The paper from the community hall.

'I'm afraid I can't.'

Kay was still talking, but Slim lowered the phone to his lap and stared off into space. He could still hear a faint voice as he put down the phone and picked up the brandy instead.

52

'I'VE TOLD YOU, YOU CAN'T DRINK IN THE COMMUNITY hall.'

'I'm not in it,' Slim said, his voice little more than a slur. 'I'm sitting on the step outside. It's raining. I'm getting wet.' He gestured to the damp patches on his knees which were catching a trickle from a crack in the guttering overhead. For the last half an hour he'd been watching the trickle of water soak first one leg, then, after an adjustment, the other, finding a strange sense of comfort in the action's regularity.

'Well, why aren't you in it?' Mandy said. 'It's freezing out here.'

'I couldn't get the door to open.'

'That's because it's on a latch. You have to lift it up first before you turn the handle. How much have you had to drink?'

Slim lifted the bottle. 'Is there anything left inside?'

'Doesn't look like it.'

'Then all of it.'

Mandy sighed. 'Come on, let's get you inside and dried off. You can use the hand-dryer in the toilet to dry your jeans. But if you're sick in there, I swear I'll rub your face in it.'

'I won't be,' Slim said. 'I was already sick over there.'

'Where?'

Slim pointed. 'There. That verge.'

Mandy sighed. 'Come on, get up.'

She helped Slim inside. A few minutes later, with Mandy mothering him in a way that could serve as practice for her own impending parenthood, Slim found himself sitting at a table with a strong coffee, nursing down a plate of dry digestive biscuits which Mandy claimed would 'soak up whatever's still in there.'

Nearby, his jeans hung over a chair in front of a radiator and a towel lay over his legs. The spinning sensation was beginning to ease.

'Thanks,' he said as Mandy came in, carrying an empty bucket.

'You can't see it anymore,' she said, holding up the bucket. 'I washed it into the ditch. What were you eating? Looked like Plymouth city centre on a Friday night out there.'

Slim shrugged. 'Beans.'

'I suppose at least you're getting some nutrition. Do you always drink like this?'

Slim shrugged. 'Off and on. And when I'm stressed.'

'What's stressing you now?'

'I'm being stalked by a dead man,' Slim said. 'But I'm not sure why.'

Mandy smiled, perhaps thinking it was a joke. 'Sounds like that movie *Ghost*. The one with Demi Moore and Patrick whatshisname. I watched it last Christmas. He was trying to tell her something. Perhaps that's what your ghost is doing.'

Slim sighed. 'Maybe.'

'I've gotta clean the kitchen. You stay here.'

Slim nodded. What if Mandy was right? What could it be?

He still had the three dolls in his pocket, the one Shelly had thrown, and the two found outside his cottage. He pulled them out, looking them over. Two men and a burned boy. Two men ... he frowned.

Kay's words: *the way you interpret things isn't always the same as the rest of us.*

One was slightly haphazard, it's limbs not straight. And the tuft of white hair ... he looked closer. It hung around the figure's neck but there was a spot of glue on the body where it had come detached.

Not a man.

A sheep.

One man, a sheep, a burned boy.

They had to be connected. Dennis, from beyond whatever he called a grave, was attempting to tell Slim something.

'I need to make a phone call,' Slim said.

He stumbled outside. Standing under the covered porch, he called Don.

'Slim! I've been trying to call you.'

'Sorry, Don, I got held up. I have another request. So sorry, I'll owe you hugely for all of this. I wondered if you could look into something else for me. It's about the abattoir again.'

'That's why I was calling. I found something. This could be massive, Slim.'

Slim felt a prickle of excitement race up his arms. 'Go on.'

'It came about at random. I was just watching some TV doc about crap farming practices … anyway, I got this idea and I changed tack. I stopped searching published material and went looking for stuff that fell under the radar. I got in touch with some editors from conservation journals, things like that. And one came up with the money.'

'What do you mean?'

'Way back in 1998, a journal called *Eco Survival* had a sub from a Devon-based environmentalist claiming that a certain Devonshire abattoir had allowed a chemical called CHT to leach into the groundwater. Used as a steriliser in meat production, it's now officially on a banned substances list. However, back then, it was considered potentially hazardous if not contained adequately. This guy claimed a spill of by-product had leached into groundwater, causing cancerous growths in sheep drinking from local streams and also possibly affecting the wells providing drinking water for more than a dozen local families. The man argued that the abattoir be held liable and accountable.'

'And what happened?'

'There were flaws in his science, issues with the content. He was asked to rewrite parts of it and resubmit. He never did.'

'Why not?'

'He died.' A long pause. 'Cancer.'

'Did the journal know?'

Don laughed. 'The editor had no idea until I told him on a return call. I rang around hospitals, pulled some strings.'

'You have the man's name?'

'Yes, of course. I hope you're sitting down, Slim. The man's name was Julian Sharp, Dennis's father.'

53

MANDY HAD GONE HOME. SLIM, RAPIDLY SOBERING UP, was glad for the quiet as he searched the library for the information he needed.

A topographical map had the wells clearly marked. Four in all, and it was obvious from their general locations which houses they had serviced.

One had serviced Shelly's old cottage. Another was right under Kenny Kent's property.

The pictures of Colin Kent made sense now. He wasn't thin, he was sick.

Dennis Sharp had known, and he had known the Ozgood family was somehow responsible for the boys' deaths.

A cover-up, exposed in tableaux, right in front of Ozgood's face.

Slim couldn't see the full display in the pictures, but he could see enough. Figurines of dead kids, cancerous sheep, and there, to one side, two men with blue shirts holding another man dressed in black.

An expose, a taunt.

The net's closing, Oliver, that tableaux said. *Your time is coming.*

Slim checked the dates. December the 22nd. The same night of Sharp's supposed death. Had the man arguing with him been Ollie Ozgood?

Yet Sharp had somehow survived the crash, and was now hiding out, slowly slipping clues to Slim.

He frowned. It still didn't make complete sense. Who was the blackmailer? Was it someone working with Dennis Sharp?

Croad, perhaps?

Slim's phone rang. As though thought-police were on his tail, Croad's number flashed up.

'What?'

'Mr. Ozgood called again. He wants a conference call with you tonight. He wants answers. We have three days. Do you have anything?'

Slim hesitated. Croad was the last person he wanted to trust.

'Yeah, I do. I have proof Dennis is alive.'

'What proof?'

Fingering the doll in his pocket, Slim said, 'Pick me up in an hour from outside the church.'

'What are you doing there?'

'Just pick me up.'

Slim could almost see Croad scowling.

'All right.'

Slim headed for Kenny Kent's place. A light was on

inside the cabin. As Slim entered through the gate he saw a metal pipe half a metre wide sticking out of the ground with a tin lid fitted and bolted over the top. An old well, the rust and sealed pipe fixtures showing it was no longer used.

The car was gone but a figure moved about inside the cabin. Slim went in without knocking, disturbing Jimmy Kent, who was dragging a bookcase across the floor.

'Jimmy.'

'What the hell do you want?'

'Is your dad about?'

Jimmy stood up straight, puffing out his chest like a bird preening its feathers. He clenched his fists and advanced towards Slim with a scowl on his face.

'You've got a nerve coming here.'

'Save it. I don't have time for this. I need to talk to your dad. It's about your brother.'

Jimmy's brow furrowed, almost covering his eyes. He pouted as though chewing gum, and took another step closer.

'What about him?'

'That's for me and your father to discuss. When will he be back?'

'Nothing you can say to him you can't say to me. Why don't you just get lost? My dad doesn't need you bringing up all this.'

'Jimmy, it's important. When will he be back?' When Jimmy just stared, Slim added, 'I know all about him.'

'You bastard, coming around here telling all your lies—'

Jimmy leapt forward, right arm swinging. Slim had expected it and was waiting. He stepped in towards Jimmy's midriff, lowering his centre of gravity, and elbowed Jimmy in the stomach as the younger man's punch glanced harmlessly off his shoulder.

Jimmy collapsed to the ground, winded. He stared up at Slim with eyes full of hate as he gasped for breath.

'God knows what that girl sees in you,' Slim said, shaking his head. 'Do you know she's pregnant?' he added, hoping Mandy would later forgive him. Jimmy's eyes widened as though he thought Slim was making it up, but Slim was on a roll. 'It seems she's getting responsible,' he snapped. 'Perhaps you could try doing the same. Or if you're going to blow your own head off, at least find something with some potency.'

'What do you want from my family?' Jimmy wheezed.

'Answers, and confirmation. Tell me if you know anything. We don't have to involve your dad at all.'

'What?'

'Colin didn't look much like you, did he?' Jimmy's scowl was replaced by a look of surprise. 'Did your dad know?'

Jimmy's expression changed again, this time puckering up as though he might start to cry.

'He figured it out later. After Colin died. The bitch left a note before she went and left us.'

'What bitch?'

'My mum. I didn't know at the time, but years later, one night after he'd had a few, Dad told me what she did.'

Slim kept his gaze steady. 'Colin was sick, wasn't he?'

'How'd you figure all this out?'

'It was easy once I realised what I was looking at. What was it? What did he have?'

Jimmy looked away. 'Leukemia,' he said, staring at the floor. 'He was having treatment but it wasn't looking good. Dad said once that the fire might have been a mercy. A lot quicker than it might have been.'

'And your mum, she couldn't get over it?'

Jimmy winced, squeezing his eyes shut. A tear dribbled down his cheek. 'She jumped off the overpass.'

'You think she failed you.'

'I don't think anything. I was a seven-year-old kid. I needed her too.'

Slim stared at Jimmy, hating himself for dredging up such misery. He closed his eyes, taking a deep breath, throwing off his own regrets, trying to focus.

'So you know what it's like, don't you? Being without a parent? You want to let history repeat itself?'

Jimmy opened his eyes. The malice had gone, replaced by a look of resignation.

'Pregnant,' he muttered.

'I'm guessing it's yours.'

Jimmy looked up at him. 'Why'd you bring all this up? All this about my brother? What has it got to do with you?'

'I don't think your brother got the justice he deserved.'

'And what, you're like some Lone Ranger come to serve it up? Look at you, you're just an old drunk in a duffel coat.'

Slim nodded. 'Then make it your life's ambition not to end up like me.' He took a step closer to the door. 'No need to tell your dad I called. You told me everything I needed to know.' He turned towards the door then paused, looking back. 'For what it's worth, which I know isn't much, I'm sorry.'

Jimmy stared at him but said nothing. Slim turned and let himself out, walking away into the cold.

54

Cathy rubbed her eyes, wiping away a tear. 'Who the hell are you, coming round here saying all this stuff?'

Slim gave her a tired smile. 'I'm an old drunk in a duffel coat.'

Cathy shook her head. 'Well, I guess it doesn't matter now, does it? The games club, Mary never missed a week. The affair was long over, although from what she said, it had only ever been a silly fling, but she felt it her duty to let Dennis see his son. Colin, he didn't know, of course. He might have by now if he had lived.'

'She confided in you?'

Cathy sighed, sniffing back more tears. 'Some, not everything. I knew she'd fallen out of love with Kenny years before, but Jimmy was Kenny's son and she couldn't bear to break up the family.'

'Did you know she was going to kill herself?'

Cathy buried her face in her hands. 'Oh, Slim, I sometimes wish you'd never shown up. I've never spoken of any of this, not even to Tom. I knew she was low after Colin's death. She was heartbroken. She came to me, desperate, after a row with Kenny. He suspected, and he'd asked her straight out. She couldn't bring herself to tell him, so she'd run off. I told her to go back, to sort it out. She agreed, but she never did. She went to that damn bridge. She left a note in her handbag, sealed, addressed to Kenny.'

'I'm sorry.'

Cathy looked up at him. 'Why did Ozgood have to call you? All of this is buried, over. We've moved on.'

Slim swallowed. 'Not everyone has,' he said.

Cathy let out a gasp then aimed a slap at him. He took a step back to avoid it.

'What are you trying to prove?' she said under her breath.

'Can I speak to your husband?'

Cathy frowned. 'What? Tom?'

'If he's back from work, yes please.'

'I don't see what....' Cathy continued to stare at him as she trailed off. 'Slim, no, please don't tell me....'

'Can I speak with him?'

Cathy gave a silent nod. She went back through the curtain and Slim heard a couple of doors open and close. Cathy was gone a long time, but when she finally returned, heavy footfalls followed behind hers.

Cathy appeared through the curtain. A shadow appeared behind her, materialising into the figure of a man, a clear head taller and broader too, the kind of body that could haul a heavy sheep carcass out of the maintenance door at the back of an abattoir, across a field and down into a wood.

'Tom Jenkins,' he said in a deep voice. He shook Slim's hand in a powerful grip.

Slim looked up into his eyes. 'Thank you for not giving up,' he said.

Cathy frowned. 'What's this about, Tom?'

Slim didn't break his gaze. 'Did you know I saw you that day?'

'When?'

'A couple of weeks back. I think it was a Tuesday. Right after lunch. I only saw your uniform but when I got hold of the profiles I knew it had to be you. Of those I couldn't find online, four were women and the fifth was a sixty-four-year-old man. Tough for a guy that age to do what you did.'

Tom stared at the ground like a school kid caught stealing.

'I had no choice.'

Cathy took his arm, leaning around to look up into his face. 'Tom? Have you met Slim before?'

As Tom gave a sullen shake of the head, Slim said, 'The groundwater's still infected, isn't it? How many have you found?'

Tom's stature betrayed the defeat in his eyes. As Cathy watched him open-mouthed, he shook his head again.

'Four this year. Two cancer, one stomach ulcer, one with polyps in the digestive tract. All four had access to the same water supply. The wells might be closed but the groundwater still shows the spill's impact.'

Slim nodded. 'And you hide them.'

Tom looked pained. 'I don't know what else to do.'

Cathy said, 'You told me you'd stopped! And after what happened to Dennis, Tom, I thought we agreed—'

Slim stilled her with a hand on her arm. 'Sometimes we can't give something up, even when we want to, even when we know it would be for the best. Believe me, I know that better than anyone.' Then, turning to Tom, he said, 'You're saving them for something.'

'I can't just let them go out to sale. Who knows what could be in that meat? But who would listen to me? Vincent's is a closed shop. They're all either in his pocket or Ellie's. I hide them because I don't know what else to do.'

'Dennis had a plan, didn't he? He had a contact.'

Tom nodded. 'He never told me who. But after he died, it never felt right to stop. I carried on in his memory. And I couldn't just forget what those bastards had done.'

'I have contacts,' Slim said. 'I can find someone who can analyse those carcasses, look for a connection.'

At last Tom looked up. 'The spill happened in 1994,' he said. 'They knew that stuff was borderline, but as the regs came close to passing the price of existing stock plummeted. They bought it up to save a few quid. Huh, not like the Ozgoods' to do that, is it?'

'You saw what happened?'

'I was fresh out of school, working in haulage. Lorry bringing the stuff in round the back hit a rut. Ten barrels fell off, broke open. Most spilled into the ditch. Sure, once the fumes had eased they had us clean it up, but it was too late. It had leached into the ground. Oliver was between tours, lording it like Ellie does now. Gave us a payoff, told us to shut our mouths.'

'And you did?'

Tom shrugged. 'It wasn't until years later when Dennis came to see me, that I even thought about it. He wanted a man on the inside.'

'You knew him?'

'Same class at school. Though he was hardly ever there. Always off running around the woods. Boy could hardly read or write but he could identify a species of mushroom at a hundred yards.'

Slim sighed. 'This is a mess.'

'Not wrong,' Cathy said. 'Not what you were hired to uncover, I expect.'

Slim turned to Tom. 'I was hired by Oliver Ozgood to uncover the identity of a blackmailer. In a roundabout way, I think I've done that.'

The look in Tom's eyes took a moment to change. 'What … you don't think…?'

Slim held his gaze for a few seconds then shook his head. 'I did, until I saw your reaction. I've interrogated possible terrorists. It's hard to learn how to hide guilt. Most people can't do it, and if there's no guilt there, it's easy to see.'

Tom glared at him. 'I'd be happy to see Ozgood behind bars for a long time. Otherwise, I want nothing from him. Getting the Ozgood family cloud away from Scuttleworth would be enough.'

Slim nodded. 'Then it seems I need to look elsewhere. I'll be in touch.'

55

SLIM SAT IN FRONT OF A LAPTOP IN THE KITCHEN OF Ozgood Hall. Even here the connection was far from perfect, so the lights had been dimmed as though that would make the exchange clearer. On the screen, however, even though Ollie Ozgood's picture was a little pixilated, his expression was easy enough to read. He looked flustered, frustrated. He glared into a device at his end then continued pacing up and down the inside of a hotel room, the walls and occasional glimpse of a window flickering behind his profile.

'So, you have no concrete proof of anything. You say you saw Sharp, but what did you see really? A tramp, a traveller? What am I paying you for? Where are the pictures? The evidence? A few wooden dolls lying around?'

Slim hadn't told Ozgood the specifics of what he had found, only that Sharp had left some woodcraft items for him to find.

'I think he's trying to contact me,' Slim said. 'But for whatever reason, he's afraid.'

'Yet he's not afraid to take my money and threaten my family?'

'His character is a hard one to figure out, I'll admit.'

Ozgood stopped pacing and turned to face the camera.

'I have come to a regrettable decision. Less than forty-eight hours from now, I must leave a bag of money for Dennis Sharp. I refuse to be blackmailed, but I will offer an olive leaf. A partial settlement, and a note. One asking for discussion, compromise. I cannot wait any longer.'

'And what should I do during this transaction?'

'You?' Ozgood laughed. 'You'll be gone. I paid for a result, but I got none. I expect your bags packed and you off my property by ten o'clock tomorrow morning. Croad will drive you to the nearest bus or train station if you so wish.'

'But I'm close to a breakthrough.'

'Not close enough. I have no patience for time wasters, Mr. Hardy. And Kay Skelton talked so highly of your detective skills.'

'We need to discuss a fee.'

Ozgood laughed. 'What fee? I ordered a job done. It wasn't done. From what Croad tells me, you've done little but wander around drunk and get in fights with the locals.'

'I've been here more than three weeks!'

'And I imagine having a roof and free food was of some comfort, wasn't it?'

Slim glared at the computer screen but kept his mouth shut. He had nothing to gain by berating Ozgood now. The smart option was to take his sanity and run.

'Forget tomorrow,' he said, throwing a glance at Croad, standing to the left in the shadows behind the laptop's screen, arms folded, eyes down. 'I'll be out tonight.'

56

CROAD OFFERED HIM A LIFT BACK FROM OZGOOD Hall to collect his stuff, but Slim refused. It was dark outside and he was desperate for a drink, so he walked in the opposite direction of where he might find one, taking winding lanes that led away from Ozgood Hall, stumbling through potholes in the darkness, letting his mind drift, not wanting to think about the case, but at the same time unable to get it out of his head. It was a jigsaw, all the pieces lying on the ground but some missing the pictures, others with the connecting nodes cut off, leaving Slim uncertain as to where they might fit. He was so close, he knew it, yet the answer lay just out of reach.

He didn't know how long he'd been walking, but the chill had set in by the time the roar of cars on the duel carriageway appeared and he found himself walking out onto the bridge where, on November 9th at 5.25 p.m, just under three days from now, the ghost of Dennis

Sharp was expecting to pick up two million pounds in used banknotes, or threaten an exposé that would destroy the Ozgood family's reputation.

His head told him to walk away and not look back, but his heart was so entangled in the knot of Scuttleworth's community that he had passed a point of no return.

He counted along the pillars from the start of the bridge, and stopped by pillar number nine. With a long sigh, he turned and looked back at the lights of Ozgood Hall on the hill in the distance.

In his pocket he had his old Nokia phone and a wallet containing an ATM card that didn't work, along with a crumpled handful of bank notes from the last time it had. Everything Slim owned in the world. He had left behind the equipment Alan had sent, but he could pay that off later. There was nothing to stop him walking off across the bridge and never looking back.

Slim took a deep breath, thinking about Mary Kent, who had jumped to her death from this very spot. If he walked away, her death, that of her son Colin, and numerous others, would be for nothing.

With another sigh, he turned and started walking back in the direction of Scuttleworth.

Clora sounded surprised but she buzzed him in anyway. As he reached the top of the stairs, breathing heavily under the weight of two large canvas bags, she sat up in her chair and fixed him with a bemused look. She was wearing pajamas, but otherwise everything about her was the same.

'And to what do I owe this unexpected visit? You do know it's almost midnight?'

Slim put down his bags, took a moment to gather his breath, and then said, 'I need a place to stay for a couple of nights. Three at the most. I'll be gone by Tuesday, I promise.'

Clora lifted an eyebrow. 'Why me?'

Slim smiled. 'Because of everyone I've encountered in Scuttleworth, you're the one who hates me the least.'

57

CLORA SEEMED HAPPY TO HAVE A HOUSE GUEST. THE next morning, she kindly allowed Slim to make them both breakfast then instructed him to shift aside a pile of boxes to make a proper space for his things. Just after ten o'clock she informed him of some shows she needed to watch, and as he wanted to make a couple of phone calls, he made himself scarce, heading back up to the village.

A light rain was falling. Slim sheltered in the church porch while he called Don.

'Thanks as always, mate,' he said. 'Things are going well, but I still need a couple more things figured out. This might sound strange, but can you try to find out if a man called Thomas Croad was on the books at QPR back in the Eighties, when they were still a decent team?'

Don laughed. 'That's one of your strangest for sure, but I'll do my best to get back to you this aft.'

'Appreciated.'

Slim hung up. Next he tried to call Kay but received no answer. He sighed, wondering what to do. He wanted to go and see Cathy, perhaps apologise for his accusations against Tom, but he could only see it going the wrong way. Instead he headed to the community hall. Pleased to find it empty, he pulled out a folder from his bag of all the documents he had taken from his table. Among them were the photocopies of the letters supposedly sent by Dennis Sharp to Ollie Ozgood. Slim stared at them, compelling them to reveal some clue, but nothing jumped out. Who was playing the game now, and who was keeping the clues?

His phone rang. Kay.

'Slim? Good to hear from you. I was worried after the other day.'

'I screwed up, Kay. Sorry. I'm back on the wagon for a while now. I think. While you're on the line, I need another favour. It's a big one, I'm sorry. Do you know anyone who works specifically with toxic chemicals?'

Kay laughed. 'You don't ask for much, Slim.'

'I know. Any chance?'

Kay sighed. 'Not offhand, but I'll do some reaching out.'

'Thanks. One more question. You were in the military with Ollie Ozgood. You told me he left, but I heard he did another tour.'

'He could have done. I don't know. Again, I can ask some questions.'

'What was his specialty? Do you know?'

'Easy one. Radios. He was an operator, but also on

237

maintenance detail. We always joked it was because he was scared of the front line.'

'Maintenance?'

'Yeah, things used to break a lot out there in the desert. Half the time he'd be sat in a room back at base rewiring stuff that had frayed.'

Slim gave a thoughtful nod. 'If you find out, please call me. I'm running down to the wire here.'

'Is that a joke?'

'I wish it was.'

'Be careful, Slim. Ollie Ozgood is not a man I would ever trust.'

'Don't worry, we're a long way past that stage.'

Slim hung up, returning to the letters. There had to be some clue to the blackmailer's identity. A single slip, perhaps a misused word.

Another resident had left a copy of yesterday's newspaper open on the puzzles page, a crossword and some word anagram puzzle partially filled in. Slim stared at it, wishing the Ozgood mystery could be so straightforward, so streamlined, then turned back to the letters, thinking of puzzles, staring at the words, wishing some clue would reveal itself.

He hadn't realised how tired he was until his eyes began to droop. His vision blurred, the words losing their meanings, standing out at irregular intervals from the page in unusual orders like the keys of an inversed typewriter.

And then he saw it.

'Oh my god,' he whispered.

58

'Is that something Den would have said?'

Clora stared at the line of text Slim had scribbled on a piece of paper.

Don't forget how you hurt me.

Clora shrugged. 'I think you're clutching at straws, but it makes a good puzzle.'

'It fits,' Slim said. 'Someone left a newspaper open on the puzzles page, and it got me thinking about hidden codes. Cryptic stuff, the kind of thing you might hide in a Valentines' card at school to a girl you liked. I read the words down the side, tried some combinations of numbers. A couple of words seemed not to fit with the tone of the previous letters. I tried a couple of combinations, some dates and times, and one fit.'

'Okay….' Clora was frowning. 'Run that past me again.'

'Tomorrow,' Slim said. 'The blackmailer's assigned drop-off time. November ninth, at five twenty-five.' He took a pen from a table beside the sofa and wrote out a date and time in numbers:

9/11. 5.25.

Then, he wrote them again as a simple line of digits:

9/1/1/5/2/5.

'It's the same time and date as the drop off. Now look at the words I've underlined and see what sentence they spell. It can't surely be a coincidence.'

He held out a copy of the letter.

Dear Oliver,
This is your last chance to settle up. Don't
forget what you did to Scuttleworth, or
how many lives you destroyed.
It is time for you to pay for
the hurt you caused. I've given you
a chance to help me make amends.
9th November, 5.25pm.
A black leather bag tied to the ninth pillar.
See you then.
Dennis

'It's a bit flukey, isn't it?'

'But it fits. What if this date is significant to Dennis, or whoever he's working with?' Clora rolled her eyes. 'You still think he's alive, don't you?'

'Evidence suggests it, and there's what I've seen with my own eyes.'

'Slim, I've known you barely a month and even I can tell you have a habit of misreading things. What's this proof?'

'Here.'

Slim pulled the dolls out of his pocket. 'Shelly threw the first one at me, but the other two—the sheep and the burned boy—were left outside the cottage for me to find.'

'By who?'

'Dennis. I got it on video.'

Clora looked skeptical. 'Show me,' she said. 'I knew Dennis as well as anyone.'

Slim pulled his laptop out of a bag, opened it, and loaded the recorded feed. He pressed play and Clora frowned as the figure of Dennis Sharp appeared on screen, moving up the path and stopping low by the front door.

'See?'

Clora shook her head. 'Can you zoom it in? I spend way more time staring at a screen than you do. I mean, those look like his clothes and he has the right build, but there's no decent shot of his face.'

'What about the doll?'

Clora frowned. 'Rewind it again.' When Slim repeated the shot, Clora said, 'Watch his hand as he bends down. You can just see it as he pulls it out of his pocket.'

'It's too blurry.'

'Yeah, but you can see the greens of the trees in the background beside his fingers. Look closer.'

Slim squinted at the screen. 'What are you seeing?'

'Nothing, that's the point. His hand's empty.' Clora looked up. 'He's not putting that doll down. He's picking it up.'

Slim stared at her, then replayed the video. It was difficult to see, but there was a chance she was right.

'Do you have any footage before that?'

'The camera got knocked by a bird and it was swaying. That's the only shot I got.'

'You only had one camera? What kind of detective are you?'

'I had another, but it showed the back of the house.'

'Let me see.'

Slim opened up the recorded feed and rewound it to the same approximate time. It had been tripped multiple times, all by birds.

'Go back further,' Clora said. 'You can see the road past the side of the house. If someone came from Scuttleworth they would have come down that way.'

Slim did as she asked. Thirty minutes before Dennis's appearance, the camera had triggered. A shuffling figure in a coat appeared out of the trees, walking slowly down the road. The feed cut out as the figure moved in front of the house's front corner, then it came back on again a couple of minutes later to show the figure walking back up the road.

'I told you,' Clora said. 'I mean, it was obvious from the look of those dolls. Dennis was a craftsman, his figurines were amazing. These look like they were made by a kid.'

'Who was that?' Slim asked.

'Don't you know? Come on, Slim. That was *her*, wasn't it? She wanders about from time to time. These dolls aren't a message from Dennis. They're from his mother, Shelly.'

59

CLORA SAID THE LARGE RAIN COAT HAD BELONGED TO Dennis. It certainly kept the rain off and would make him harder to spot from a distance. Afraid of being seen by Croad, Slim cut through the woods to get to Harton, the journey killing too much time, but when he arrived, the small library was still open. He headed straight for the collection of local papers, going back a few years and trawling through them for anything he had overlooked before.

It was amazing, he thought, how something so obvious could remain in plain sight without being seen, but even though he felt sure the pieces were falling into place, he still didn't know how he could land a killing blow and close the case once and for all. Too many questions still burned.

The journey back to Scuttleworth was a long and arduous one. Slim, buoyed by his discoveries but still weighed down by a healthy dose of fear, had been unable to resist buying a small bottle from the village shop before starting the journey. Now, as he slogged up the hill to Scuttleworth, he was drunk and soaked through.

The village presented a mythical tapestry of buildings slowly emerging out of the fog. Slim went first to Cathy's shop, but the lights were off and a CLOSED sign sat in the window. The lights in the house behind were also off, so Slim headed for the community hall. Here, lights blazed through the windows, and a crack in the curtains revealed a badminton game in full flow, its players no one Slim recognised. Feeling as alone as he ever had, he walked away from the indication that life would go on long after his investigation was over, heading for the church.

As he approached Shelly's tent, for the first time Slim was glad he was drunk. He hoped that she might recognise a kindred spirit in this drunken, failing man, but if not, he kept his hands up just in case, wary of any further projectiles.

'Shelly, it's Slim,' he said. 'I'm sorry to bother you, but I wanted to say thanks for bringing me those dolls. You helped me a lot, and I hope some good might come of it.'

No answer. Slim took a couple of steps closer, reaching out tentatively for the tent flap. He held his free hand across his face as he lifted it, allowing the glow from a street light on the churchyard's edge to search inside.

On a camp bed against the back wall Shelly lay, her

hands under her face, a blanket covering her body. She looked for all the world as though she were sleeping, except that her eyes were wide open, staring sightlessly out at the churchyard, seeing something in death that may have been her last view in life.

60

Slim heard the sirens as he stumbled through the woods in the rough direction of Ozgood Hall. He had felt it his duty to make an anonymous call, but had gone off-road to avoid being seen by any police or medical services.

His phone buzzed. Don's voice was crackly, on the verge of cutting out.

'Found him. Thomas Croad, made a few dozen appearances for QPR's reserves between '85 and '89. Never quite made the cut, and lost his contract for '90. I could find no further trace after that.'

'Thanks, Don.'

Slim hung off before the poor reception cut him off anyway. The rain had returned, and as he slipped and slid down the leafy slope in near darkness, Slim soon found himself scratched and soaked. His sense of direction was long gone, helped only by the sound of the occasional car on the lanes through the trees.

He wasn't sure how he found Den's old car, but somehow he did. He leaned against the rusted remains of the bonnet to catch his breath then pulled his phone out of his pocket.

The tiny light was barely an improvement on the darkness, but it was something, and after a few seconds of letting his eyesight adjust, it seemed brighter than a regular torch.

Pushing aside the undergrowth, he climbed through the open door and sat down on the passenger seat, wincing as what was left of the sponge released its water load to soak his back and upper legs.

No matter. The brandy would keep him warm.

He leaned across to the driver's side, pulling up the seat and shining his phone light on the space below. As he had expected, he saw a device attached to the springs, a little switch activated by compression, leading to a wire feeding out through the floor, most likely to a set of speakers hidden a short way off into the woods. Of course, it had long since broken, the wire rusted through, but the little device activating a faint microphone must have worked long enough to put the fear of god into the local kids, long enough for a player of games to have his fun.

Slim switched off his phone, slipped it back into his pocket, and leaned back, letting the rain soak him.

'Come on, Dennis,' he said. 'I know you're out there. I've heard you following me. No point hiding any longer. We're fast coming up on the end.'

At first the crunch of footfalls was barely audible over the patter of the rain. Then a silhouette appeared by the bonnet of the car, outlined against grey sky visible through the leafless trees. Not a ghost but certainly a man as it felt its way around to the driver's side.

Slim heard soft breathing as the man climbed in beside him. He stared straight ahead into the gloom then pulled the bottle out of his coat, jostling the trickle of brandy left inside.

'I saved you some,' Slim said, holding the bottle up.

The figure shifted beside him. 'I don't drink,' a man's voice said. 'Like a lot of things, it's a fool's game.'

There was a rustle of movement then a thud, and as Slim toppled sideways, his vision wavering, he became aware that something hard and blunt had struck him in the side of the head.

61

THE FIRST THING SLIM REALISED UPON WAKING WAS that the rain had stopped. The second was that it was no longer night, and that the sun was far overhead.

He tried to move but his hands were tied behind him, and from the numbing ache all over his body it was clear he had lain motionless for several hours. His bladder was bursting and one side of his body felt damp and warm where he had lain on the water soaking his clothes. The upper side, where they had begun to dry in the cold sun, was achingly cold.

'It didn't have to be this way.'

Slim shifted to look in the direction of the voice. Oliver Ozgood sat at a foldout table nearby, smoking a cigarette and apparently reading a newspaper.

'I gave you the chance to walk away. All you had to do was leave.'

'I'm surprised to see you,' Slim said. 'I still thought there was a chance I was hunting Dennis Sharp. After all, I know you never saw him dead. You were just trying to scare me, keep me in line the way you attempted to keep the whole of Scuttleworth in line. I know, because you weren't even in the country at the time of the crash.'

Ozgood rolled his eyes. 'A great detective at work, eh? You pulled my bank records.'

Slim shook his head. 'I searched the tabloids. You were a little more popular six years ago than now. The public used to care about you. Pictures of you on your holidays, sitting on your yacht. Like a proper famous person, eh?'

Ozgood shrugged.

'And what else, in your mastery, did you figure out?'

Slim craned his head, trying to see around him. It appeared he was lying in the clearing outside the hut he had mistakenly assumed was Dennis Sharp's hideout.

'What are you going to do with me?' he said.

'I'll think of something.'

'You can't just leave me here.'

'Why not? It was hard enough for a military man like you to find this place. You could lie here for years without being discovered.'

'Why not just let me go? Nothing I have on you would stick.'

'I did tell you that, didn't I? I could make it all go away.'

Slim decided to change tack. Ozgood held all the advantage. All he had was his old military negotiation skills, but even back in the day they had been rudimentary at best.

'I didn't prove to be a great detective, did I?'

Ozgood shook his head. 'To be fair, I expected better. I also suspected that, like your life, you might deviate. That's why I stuck around. To keep an eye on you.'

'Dressing in Dennis's old work clothes to create a little confusion if I spotted you.'

Ozgood shrugged. 'There were some left in the old workshop, and I had nothing I wanted to get dirty. And we were about the same size.'

'Why did you kill those kids? They did nothing to you. Colin would have died soon anyway.'

Ozgood stood up. He marched towards Slim, his face darkening. Slim knew he was pushing his luck, but part of him was interested to see how far Ozgood would go. He sensed that he'd already be dead if that was Ozgood's plan.

The kick was hard enough to wind Slim, but then Ozgood stepped back, circling around, smashing at the undergrowth with his hands.

'If you had a family name you might understand,' he said. 'But you, you don't even have a proper first name.'

'No one was around so you went in there and set that fire, didn't you?'

Ozgood stared at the ground. 'No.'

'Then what?'

Ozgood didn't turn around. His shoulders lifted and fell, his breath coming in huge, ragged gasps. 'I went there looking for Shelly. She was late on her rent, as always. I knew not to waste my time pestering Dennis, because he didn't care.'

'So that explains things. You went in there to rough her up a bit. You, an ex-marine, and Shelly a sickly old hippy. Tough guy, aren't you?'

'Says the man tied up on the ground.'

'You scared the kids upstairs then set the fire.'

Ozgood turned around. His eyes glistened with tears. 'You think you know so much, don't you?'

'Then tell me, Oliver. Tell me what I don't know.'

Ozgood stared at the ground. He grimaced, his lower lip trembling, his brow furrowed as though his face might suddenly crumple and fall to the ground like an autumn leaf.

'The house was old,' he muttered. 'I thought … I thought it would teach Shelly a lesson not to screw my father around. The fuse box was a mess. It only took a couple of sparks. I was in and out in a couple of minutes.' He looked down at his feet, clenching his fists, his chest heaving with sobs. 'I didn't … know … they … were … there.'

Slim closed his eyes a moment, feeling a heavy lump of sorrow landing on his chest. Then, remembering everything else this man had done, he opened his eyes and fixed Ozgood with a stare.

'And you blamed Dennis for not rescuing them? For not being there when he should have been there, because he had sneaked off to hide another infected animal carcass?'

Ozgood said nothing. He was still sobbing. Slim didn't think he'd ever seen anything more pathetic.

'That's what this is about, isn't it? Revenge on Dennis Sharp. You gave him an alibi because you knew the police couldn't pin anything on him, plus you thought it might help your own reputation. Then later you forced your daughter into accusing him of rape because you thought you could see him punished that way, but that failed too because your daughter actually loved him. And when he died for real you let it get whispered around the village that you were responsible, as you wish you had been.' Slim couldn't help but smile despite the futility of the situation. 'And now this. Ordinarily a man in your position would laugh off such an attempt at blackmail. But with Sharp's name attached, it's a whole different thing. You're treating it as though by some miracle Dennis Sharp might still be alive. You know he's dead, don't you? It took me a long time to come to that conclusion, but I don't think any man has ever been more dead than Dennis Sharp.'

Ozgood lifted his head. A slow smile spread across his face and a maniacal gleam appeared in his eyes.

'I have to make sure,' he said.

'But you know he had nothing to do with the blackmail, don't you? He's dead, you damn idiot.'

Ozgood was still staring straight ahead. 'What would you know?'

Slim wanted to laugh. 'Because out of everything, I figured that part out.'

Ozgood's smile dropped. 'You figured what?'

'The identity of the blackmailer.'

'Who?'

Slim left a dramatic pause before he whispered a

single word, but the reaction was not the one he had expected. He had expected a wry smile or perhaps a look of incredulity. Instead, there was a momentary look of sheer horror before Ozgood lifted his face to the sky and howled like a dying soldier being strafed with machine gun fire.

'*No…!*'

62

'Goddamn you bastard, move!'

Whether he felt Ozgood had the nerve to go ahead and use the hunting knife the man periodically pressed into his back, Slim wasn't sure, but Ozgood's voice had taken on a note of desperation that suggested now wasn't the time to run a test. It wasn't easy to jog through the forest with his hands tied, particularly with the recent rain turning even the slightest slope into slithering mud, but he found if he concentrated solely on the next step, he could maintain Ozgood's pace.

Seemingly intent to get all the way to the drop-off point using forest trails, Ozgood was becoming increasingly flustered as the sky darkened, the minutes ticking by.

'Just leave me behind,' Slim said. 'Tie me to a tree or something.'

'No!' Ozgood shouted, jabbing Slim hard enough this time to draw blood. Slim winced as he felt a warm trickle run down his back. 'You think I'll give you a chance to get away after everything you've done? If Ellie dies, you die.'

Ellie.

To take his mind off the numbness in his arms and the growing pain in his back from the stab wound, Slim recalled how he had finally figured it out.

The first two notes had been a teaser, with suspiciously neat handwriting and a literary prowess far more fitting for an educated young lady than someone with seemingly little education, with neat turns of phrase and unnecessarily complex words, but the third, with its crudely hidden message, had been the key. There were the clues Slim was yet to confirm, including that it had been Ellie, a besotted teenage lover during the last period of Dennis's life, who had helped him write the ledger, then there were the ones already solved.

The background: Ellie had studied cryptology as part of a mathematics course at the University of York, evidenced by a note in the local paper of her graduation —despite what Kenny Kent had claimed, Ellie had passed after all—along with a picture of a young girl with a beaming smile in a robe and mortarboard. Cryptology, the study of ciphers, their origins and creations, the kind of degree she would have had no use for in a pseudo-managerial position at Vincent's, but one that might have led her to begin the letters, a way to exercise her skills while freeing at last some of the anger she held toward her father.

Then there were the dates. September 6th, an easy one—Ellie's birthday—the missing of which had been petulantly alluded to in the second letter. October 2nd, the date of her graduation ceremony, a date on which—according to tabloid newspaper reports—Ollie had been sojourning in the Caribbean. And the one that sealed Ollie's coffin of fatherly neglect, November 9th, 2018, six years to the day when, likely cajoled by her father in his quest to soil Dennis Sharp's name, Ellie had made her initial statement to the police.

'How did you find out about Ellie and Dennis, Oliver?'

'Shut up and move!'

The knife again left a minor impression, this one a little deeper than before. Slim stumbled on a rock, just managing to keep his feet.

'Come on, Ollie, tell me,' he said. 'You spied on her, didn't you? You bugged her, just like you bugged me. I missed one, didn't I? That's how you knew when I went out.'

'In the frame over the front door,' Ozgood said. 'No one ever looks up long enough, do they?'

'Is that what you did with Ellie? And Dennis?'

Ozgood's silence felt like a confirmation.

'It must have been horrible to see her go off to university,' Slim said. 'Three years out of your control. You knew it was only a matter of time. Children are meant to fly the nest.'

'Shut your mouth!' Ozgood shouted, and this time an elbow connected with the side of Slim's face, making him stumble. 'Don't push me. Don't … push me!'

They reached a dirt road. Ozgood, breathing hard, paused to pull out his phone. He held it up into the air then gave a wild cackle. He pressed a button and held it to his ear.

'Pick up, damn you … pick up!'

With a howl of frustration he slammed his phone against his leg then kicked at a nearby bush.

'Ellie … come on….'

He tried again, but the reception was either too poor or the girl was ignoring him.

'It's getting dark,' Slim said. 'I'm slowing you down. Leave me behind.'

'No!' Ozgood shouted. He turned around, eyes blazing. He threw the phone to the ground and advanced on Slim, the knife held up. For a moment Slim feared the worst, then Ollie gave the knife a petulant swing towards Slim's shoulder, as though too afraid to go for a killing blow. Slim heard his clothes shred then felt a deep, aching pain.

'Next one's your last,' Ozgood said. 'Now move.'

With each step the pain in Slim's shoulder worsened, and blood from the wound was soaking his arm, but Ozgood had been clever to leave his legs unharmed. Despite a growing dizziness, fearful of worse, Slim quickened his pace, moving in an awkward stumble as Ozgood came behind, the prodding knife a constant reminder to keep moving. By the time he saw the glimmer of street lighting through the trees up ahead, he was at the end of his strength.

'If we don't make it, you're a dead man,' Ozgood snapped, the tremble in his voice betraying his frayed nerves.

Then they were stepping out of the trees onto the duel carriageway overpass bridge. Slim glanced back over his shoulder, at the only two distant lights visible: one outside light on the corner wall of a barn, and the other from Ellie Ozgood's bedroom window. He had mistakenly thought she was looking at the trees that night, but she had been watching the bridge, as she had undoubtedly been doing earlier today when Ollie dropped off the bag.

He turned away. There, in the darkness at the top of the gentle slope, a figure, face hidden beneath the hood of a duffel coat, was hurrying towards the ninth pillar along.

Ozgood had seen her too. 'Ellie! Stop!' he screamed, his voice cracking. 'Wait! Don't touch it!'

The figure paused a moment, half twisted to look at them, then carried on moving. On the other side of the bridge, Slim saw a car waiting, parked up against the verge.

'No, Ellie! Don't!'

The figure didn't stop. It reached over the bridge's side rail, stretching for something that had been hung over the other side.

A leather bag.

'No!'

A loud pop sounded. A small shockwave struck Slim, knocking him off his feet. From the ground he watched the figure in the jacket crumple, falling first to its knees, then dropping face first, hitting the pavement with a sharp crack, the shredded remains of the bag pluming out like the feathers of a bird struck by a car.

'Ellie!' Ozgood screamed, diving at the figure and rolling it over. Then, quieter: 'Ellie?'

A car door slammed. A lithe figure got out and came running across the bridge. A street light illuminated a young woman's pale face.

'You bastard!' Ellie screamed, aiming a kick at her father. 'You worthless bastard!'

Ollie, regaining his composure, pushed the body away and stood up.

'Ellie, I'm so glad you're safe.' He stepped towards her, reaching as though to hug her, then swung a vicious punch into her face. As she sagged to her knees, he shouted, 'You were behind this? After everything I've done for you....'

Ellie shook her head, then looked up. 'I hate you!' she screamed, jumping up, arms flailing as she attacked her father in return. 'I hate you more than anything in the world!'

While father and daughter berated each other, Slim inched back across the bridge. It was only a matter of time before they remembered him.

Below, a car roared past on the duel carriageway.

Slim nodded, his mind made up. He had one chance to get away.

As Ozgood turned and bellowed, 'Hardy!', Slim stumbled for the barrier and dived head first over the railings.

He got lucky. He was close enough to the roadside that instead of plummeting straight down to the roadway and his death, he struck a sloping embankment and rolled the rest of the way. Barely conscious, he

260

ignored a faint shout from overhead as he stumbled to his feet and staggered out into the road. As the first headlights approached he wished he had the ability to wave. The best he could do was offer a desperate shake of the head, and to his relief he saw the car slow.

As a driver got out and shouted something Slim could barely understand, he glanced up at the bridge, but both Ollie and Ellie Ozgood had gone.

EPILOGUE

Trying to read a newspaper with one arm fully casted and a smaller one on the other wrist wasn't the easiest thing Slim had ever done, but at least the hotel reception was warm and the seat beneath him soft. It was a far improvement from the bed in Derriford Hospital which had only released him two days before.

The article open in front of him was a continuing story of the trials of Oliver and Eleanor Ozgood. Ollie was set to go down for many years after admitting to two counts of involuntary manslaughter and one of voluntary, as well as numerous assault and kidnapping charges. Whether he would ever be charged for accusations relating to Vincent's was an industrial legal case that might drag on for years, but the big deal for the prosecution was proving whether the death of Shelly Holland—electrocuted by a frayed wire in her electric blanket while she slept—was murder or accidental. The case was ongoing. Meanwhile, for attempting to blackmail her own father, Ellie was likely to receive only a minimal sentence at worst. Those villagers he had spoken to had hoped she took some of her family wealth and moved far away.

'Anything interesting?' Cathy asked, appearing next to him.

Slim closed the newspaper and gave her a smile. 'Oh, not much.'

'I hear you went to Thomas Croad's funeral.'

Slim shrugged. 'I was one of only three people there, including the vicar and the nurse pushing my chair. I felt he deserved better. Ellie was as cowardly as her father for coercing him into her plan. Allegedly she didn't tell him until the morning of the deal.'

'The girl's like a spider,' Cathy said. 'In many ways Dennis Sharp had a lucky escape. No one will much miss Scuttleworth's own bogeyman. The air feels better already.' She glanced at the door. 'Oh, here they come. You need some help?'

'Please.'

Cathy took Slim's arm and helped him into the function room where the other guests were waiting. She left him near the back then headed for her family seat near the front. Jimmy stood up there beside his father, looking like a changed man in a suit and tie. He nodded at Slim then gave the briefest of smiles.

The doors opened to reveal Tom and Mandy. The girl, heavily pregnant, looked radiant in a flowing dress. Her hair was tied up, and the dyed pink strands made her look as though she wore confetti in her hair. As she passed, she glanced at Slim and mouthed, *thank you*.

Later, standing in a corner at the reception party, Slim thought about the phone call he had received from Kay a day after entering hospital. Ollie's second tour had been as part of the bomb squad. It figured that if Ollie could diffuse one, he could make one too.

Unable to drink due to medication even if he had wanted to, Slim was still standing in the corner when Kenny Kent wandered over.

'I wanted to thank you,' Kenny said. 'I don't know what you said to my boy, but I think you made a man of him. Do you think they'll last? She's only eighteen.'

Slim shrugged. 'They have as good a chance as any. I imagine it'll be tough, so the kid'll need an attentive grandfather. You'll only get a couple of years for dangerous driving if you come clean.'

Kenny looked down. 'You know it was me then?'

'Dennis wasn't much of a driver but neither Croad nor Ozgood had a vehicle which could have chased him down there. I saw what you were driving, and saw what they had available. No comparison. I asked around to see how long you'd had that four-wheel. Long enough.'

Kenny nodded, then sighed. 'I hated those Christmas festivals because they always reminded me of Mary. When I walked in to pick up Jimmy, I couldn't believe the nerve of him. The case with Ellie had only been dropped a couple of days before, and there he was, acting like the centre of the community. Even then I would probably have said nothing, but I lost it when I saw Jimmy over there by his stall. I balled Dennis out a bit, and he stormed out.' Kenny shrugged. 'I should have left it there, but I went over the pub, had a couple, and then went looking for him. I only planned to give him a bit of a slap, but when I drove down to his place, he was putting something in his car. I went after him. I trailed him for a bit and was about to give up when he went and turned down Gunhill Hollow. I followed him down and saw him go through the barrier down into the woods there.'

'Ozgood told me he called the police, but he didn't, did he? It was you.'

'I climbed down far enough to see the flames. I was a bit off my head so I panicked and left him there. Went back, called the police from outside the church on my way home. Expected them to show up the next morning but no one ever came.'

'What are you going to do now?'

'I've already called the police, said I need to have a word. An officer is coming around tomorrow.'

Slim nodded. 'I hope it goes well.'

'I made a mistake, and I deserve what I get,' Kenny said.

'There isn't a man among us who hasn't made a mistake at some point,' Slim said.

Kenny grunted as though unsure whether Slim was right or not, then moved off back into the party. It was now in full swing, a grinning Jimmy delicately leading a beaming Mandy around the dance floor.

Slim smiled. They'd be all right. Pushing himself gingerly away from the wall, he looked around the residents of Scuttleworth one last time, then turned and headed out into the night.

ABOUT THE AUTHOR

Jack Benton is a pen name of Chris Ward, the author of the dystopian *Tube Riders* series, the horror/science fiction *Tales of Crow* series, and the *Endinfinium* YA fantasy series, as well as numerous other well-received stand alone novels.

The Games Keeper is the third volume in the Slim Hardy mystery series.

Chris would love to hear from you:
www.amillionmilesfromanywhere.net/tokyolost
chrisward@amillionmilesfromanywhere.net

THANK YOU FOR READING

To learn about the next Slim Hardy book, release dates and more, visit the website of Jack Benton and Chris Ward at

www.amillionmilesfromanywhere.net

ACKNOWLEDGMENTS

Big thanks as always to those of you who provided help and encouragement. My proofreader Jenny, and the guys at The Cover Collection get a special heads up, as does as always, my muse, Jenny Twist.

In addition, extra thanks goes to my Patreon supporters, in particular to Amaranth Dawe, Charles Urban, Janet Hodgson, Juozas Kasiulis, Leigh McEwan, Teri L. Ruscak, James Edward Lee, Catherine Crispin, Christina Matthews, Alan MacDonald, and Eda Ridgeway.

You guys are awesome.

Lightning Source UK Ltd.
Milton Keynes UK
UKHW011959050722
405417UK00001B/142

9 798201 703028